SEAL SALVATION

BROTHERHOOD PROTECTORS COLORADO
BOOK #1

ELLE JAMES

TWISTED PAGE INC

SEAL SALVATION

BROTHERHOOD PROTECTORS COLORADO
BOOK #1

New York Times & USA Today
Bestselling Author

ELLE JAMES

Ebook ISBN-13: 978-1-62695-351-2

Print ISBN-13: 978-1-62695-352-9

Dedicated to my daughter who trained with the US Army at Ft. Carson, Colorado. The location is fabulous and inspired this series!
Elle James

AUTHOR'S NOTE

Enjoy other military books by Elle James

Brotherhood Protectors Colorado

SEAL Salvation (#1)

Rocky Mountain Rescue (#2)

Ranger Redemption (#3)

Tactical Takeover (#4)

Visit ellejames.com for titles and release dates

For hot cowboys, visit her alter ego Myla Jackson at mylajackson.com

and join Elle James's Newsletter at https://ellejames.com/contact/

PROLOGUE

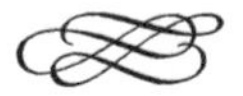

HANK PATTERSON PACED the length of the conference table in the basement of his home in Montana, muttering, "No man left behind."

"Hey boss," Axel Svenson, the giant of a Viking, ducked as he descended the steps into the headquarters of one of the finest security firms in the state of Montana.

Hank, a former Navy SEAL, had started the Brotherhood Protectors after he'd rescued movie star Sadie McClain when her bodyguards were less than effective. Since then, he'd married the movie star, had a couple of kids and hired a number of former Army, Navy and Marine special operations, highly-trained operatives, to provide security or conduct dangerous missions where the government wasn't or couldn't get involved.

He took pride in the fact he'd helped so many of

his military brotherhood find a place to fit into the civilian world.

With a large contingent of his men based in Montana, he needed to create other bases of operations. He'd set up an office in Hawaii, where former SEAL Jace "Hawk" Hawkins was the only man currently handling business there. He and some of his men had discussed other locations, including Washington, DC, New Orleans, Atlanta, New York City and Colorado.

Having grown up on a ranch, Hank liked the idea of setting up another location in an area much like his beloved Montana. Now, all he needed was to find the men to run the location.

"Hey, Hank," a familiar voice sounded from the staircase. "What's up?"

Hank lifted his chin toward Joseph "Kujo" Kuntz. "Sorry to take you away from your family on a Sunday."

Kujo descended the stairs, followed by his retired Military Working Dog, Six. "No problem. Molly had to go to her office in Bozeman to pick up some files and check in with her supervisor."

Hank smiled. "How's the pregnancy going?"

Kujo shoved a hand through his hair. "First three months were a bitch with morning sickness, but she's feeling good now."

"Will she continue to work for the FBI after the baby is born?" Hank asked.

Kujo's lips twisted, and his brow dipped. "Much

as I'd like her to quit and raise our baby, it wouldn't be fair to ask her to do that. She's good at her job."

"And you and Six are good at yours." Hank's brow rose. "You're not considering quitting, are you?"

Kujo laughed. "No way. But we're in the process of interviewing nannies."

Hank nodded. "Glad to hear it. You're a vital member of the team, here."

"Thanks," Kujo said. "I'm sure you didn't invite me here to ask about morning sickness and babies. You've got your hands full with your own children, one of which is a newborn, probably keeping you awake at night."

"Truth." Hank's smile slipped. "Think you can get away for a couple weeks before the baby is born?"

Kujo nodded slowly. "Where did you have in mind?"

Hank nodded his head toward the white board on the wall where a computer image of a state was projected. "I've got a lead on a location for our new office."

Kujo stepped closer. "New office? Where?"

"Your old stomping grounds," Hank said. "Colorado."

A grin spread across Kujo's face. "That's great." As soon as the grin came it faded. "Only, I can't be gone for long with Molly being pregnant."

Hank nodded. "I don't want you to move out there permanently. I just need you to get out there, set up shop and hire a few good men, keeping in mind that one of them will head up the location."

"I hate to be gone so long from Molly," Kujo said. "If it's okay with her, I can give you a few weeks. She's only four months along, which gives me a little time that I can be away."

"I wanted to be with Sadie every day of her pregnancy," Hank said.

"I'd like to be with Molly every day of hers. But if you need me to go to Colorado, now would be better than later this year."

Hank nodded. "Good. And I have someone in mind for leading the new team out there." His brow wrinkled. "Only he's a work in progress."

Kujo frowned. "What do you mean...work in progress?"

Hank sighed. "Not only has he lost a leg, he's lost his way."

Kujo's eyes narrowed. "I can understand. I was at my lowest when you offered me a job. If it hadn't been for you and the Brotherhood Protectors..." Kujo shook his head, his hand going automatically to Six's head.

The dog nuzzled his fingers, sensing his handler's emotions.

"I figured you of all people would see where I'm going with this. And you're from Colorado. You'll appreciate going back."

Kujo ran a hand over Six's smooth, sable head.

"You saved my life, and Six's, not long ago," Kujo said quietly.

"You and Six were worth saving. And so is Jake Cogburn."

Kujo's eyes widened. "Jake 'The Cog' Cogburn?"

Hank nodded again. "He's in a bad way, from what I hear."

"Like I was when you found me and made me rescue Six?"

"Exactly. I figured you'd have a better connection with the SEAL."

Kujo drew in a deep breath. "He has to be ready to make the change."

Hank laughed. "And you were?"

Kujo grinned. "I wasn't. But you were convincing. And knowing Six would be euthanized if I didn't go to him, motivated me."

"Cog needs someone to motivate him," Hank said. "He needs a purpose. He needs to know he's still relevant in this world."

"And you think I'm the man to pull him up by his bootstraps?" Kujo shook his head. "I don't know. Might take more than the few weeks I can give to the job."

Hank clapped Kujo on the back. "I've seen your work. I know you can handle it."

"And you want me to set up a new office for the Brotherhood Protectors?" Kujo shook his head. "That, in itself, will take some time. I'll have to find a building to rent or purchase and equip it with all the infrastructure needed." He waved his hand at Hank's basement. "This takes time."

"I have a connection near Colorado Springs." Hank turned and walked away. "He's a former Marine gunnery sergeant running a dude ranch near a small town called Fool's Gold, which is located outside of Colorado Springs." He touched several keys on a computer keyboard, and an image popped up on a screen.

Kujo looked over Hank's shoulder to view a map on the monitor.

"I think Gunny Tate's ranch has everything we need to set up shop. Great location, private enough and they need the money we'd pay in rent. It's a win-win situation. Besides, the ranch will give us the cover we need to run our operations without detection."

"Kind of like what you have here." Kujo nodded. "We're just a bunch of ranch hands, until we're given an assignment."

"Exactly." Hank's grin widened. "Gunny Tate is a character. He raised his only child singlehandedly after his wife died in childbirth. I believe that child is grown now and working the dude ranch with him. Gunny is a blustery curmudgeon with a heart of gold. Met him at McP's a million years ago after BUD/S training. His team was celebrating his transfer to a recruiting command in Colorado. He's been in Colorado ever since."

"Recruiting command?" Kujo's brows rose. "Who'd he piss off?"

Hank shook his head. "He opted to go into recruiting to end his career in a place of his choice. Being a single father raising a child, when he could be deployed at a moment's notice, wore on him. He wanted to slow down and give the child a steady home to grow up in."

"Boy or girl?" Kujo asked.

Hank grinned. "Name's Rucker. Trust Gunny to give him a tough name. I can only assume he's a boy. I never had the pleasure of meeting him."

Kujo drew in a deep breath, let it out and clapped his hands together. "When do you want me to go? This week? Next week? You name it."

Hank picked up a sheet of paper off the printer beside the monitor. "Your plane leaves at six in the morning from Bozeman and arrives in Colorado Springs before noon. That should give you plenty of time to find the town of Fool's Gold and Lost Valley Ranch. Gunny is expecting you and will take you to where Cogburn is holed up."

Kujo leaned his head toward the German Shepherd lying patiently at his feet. "What about Six?"

Hank smiled. "If you want, I can book him in the seat beside yours on the airplane."

Kujo glanced down at Six. "Guess I'm going home to Colorado. I'd like Six to stay here with Molly."

Six rose to his feet. Ready to go.

"Sorry, boy," Kujo said. "You're needed here."

Hank held out his hand. "Good luck convincing Cog we have a place for him. He was a helluva SEAL and a leader among his team. If you can pull him out of his funk, he'll make a great team leader for our Colorado location. That is, unless you'd like to take that position...?" Hank raised his eyebrows.

Kujo shook his head. "Molly's established herself at the Bozeman office of the FBI. They know her and what she's capable of. With her being pregnant, it would be a bad time to move. She'd have to start all over making her mark."

Hank nodded. "Figured as much. Besides, she has a great support system here to take care of your baby when you're both called to duty."

"Exactly. I wouldn't ask her to move now. Maybe in a year or two, but not now. I do miss Colorado. Fortunately, Montana is a lot like where I came from. Wide open spaces, blue sky, mountains and more. Here, I have a team I love working with." He shook Hank's hand. "Thanks for pulling me back into the land of the living."

"You're welcome. Now go get Cog. I have a feeling he'll be just the right fit for running the Colorado office of the Brotherhood Protectors."

As Kujo and Six left the basement conference room, Hank's gaze followed. If anyone could get Jake Cogburn to pull his head out of his ass and get to work, Kujo was the one.

"Hank?" Sadie's voice sounded from the top of the stairs.

"Yeah, babe," he responded, taking the stairs two at a time.

His beautiful wife stood with baby Mac cradled in her arms.

Hank leaned close and captured her mouth with his. "What's up, beautiful?"

She kissed him back and smiled up at him. "Is Kujo going to Colorado?"

Hank nodded. "He is."

Sadie nodded. "I'm glad. If I didn't have to show up on the set of my next film, you could go." She frowned. "I could call and reschedule."

"Don't. Kujo can handle Cog." He kissed Sadie again. "Besides, I'm looking forward to having Mac and Emma all to myself while I miss their mama."

Sadie's smile spread across her face. "I love you, Hank Patterson. And I love that you care about your former teammates enough to help them out."

He leaned back, raising his eyebrows. "Are you kidding? They're helping me. I couldn't have built this business so big and so fast without them."

Hank took Mac from Sadie's arms and carried him into the living room where Emma played with her collection of stuffed animals spread out across the area rug.

He prayed Cogburn wouldn't send Kujo packing. The man really needed a purpose for his life. If he had that, he'd realize that being short a leg wasn't the end of the world.

CHAPTER 1

JAKE COGBURN SAT in the tattered lounge chair he'd scavenged on the side of the street after moving into an empty apartment in Colorado Springs. He hadn't planned on living in an apartment, nor had he planned on sleeping on the only piece of furniture he could afford without digging into his savings. He'd put aside money to purchase a plot of land out in the middle of nowhere Colorado. On that land, he'd wanted to build a house.

All those plans had been blown away, along with the lower half of his left leg, when he'd stepped on an IED in Afghanistan. Yeah, he had the money in the bank, but what good did it do him? On one leg, what could he accomplish? Working a piece of land and building a house took all four limbs.

He poured another tumbler of whiskey and tipped the contents up, letting the cool liquid burn a path down his throat. Soon, the numbing effect set in. Jake could almost forget the phantom pain in his missing leg, could almost forget he'd not only lost a leg, but had lost the only family he'd ever had.

As a Navy SEAL, his teammates had been his brothers. Every one of them would lay down his life for him, as he'd taken one for the team when his foot had landed on that IED.

Medically discharged, having gone through multiple surgeries and physical therapy, he'd been dumped out into a civilian world that had no use for a one-legged, former Navy SEAL.

What was he good for? His skillset included demolitions, tactical operations, highly effective weapons firing and hand-to-hand combat.

Where could he find that kind of work in a civilian occupation? And doing all that balanced on one leg?

Nope.

He was all washed up. His only hope was to sit on a corner with his hat held out, begging like a hundred other homeless veterans roaming the streets of Colorado Springs.

His free hand clenched into a fist. Jake had never begged for anything in his life. He'd fought for what he'd accomplished. From surviving the gangs on the streets of Denver, to forging his way through BUD/S training, he'd always counted on his mind and brute strength to get through any hardship.

But now…

Through the empty glass tumbler, he stared down

at the stump below his left knee then slammed the glass against the wall. It hit hard and shattered into a million pieces that scattered across the floor.

A knock sounded on the door to his apartment.

"I didn't put a dent in the damned wall!" he yelled. "Leave me the fuck alone."

"Jake Cogburn?" An unfamiliar male voice called out from the other side of the faded wooden panel.

"Yeah," Jake muttered. "I'm not interested in buying anything."

"I'm not selling anything," the muffled voice sounded.

"Then get the fuck away from my door," Jake said and tipped the bottle of whiskey up, downing the last swallow. The bottle followed the glass, hitting the wall with a solid thump before it crashed to the wooden floor and bounced.

"Everything all right in there?" the man called out.

"Who the hell cares?" Jake muttered.

"I do."

Jake frowned. "I told you. I'm not buying anything."

"And I told you I'm not selling anything." A moment of silence followed. "Would you open the door for a brother?"

Anger surged through Jake. "I don't have a brother. I'm an only fuckin' child."

"Then how about a brother-in-arms? A fellow spec ops guy? A Delta Force man?"

Jake barked a single laugh. "Yeah. Yeah. Whatever.

The SEALs don't operate out of Colorado. And as far as I know, there isn't a Delta Force unit near here."

"Not active Delta Force," the man fired back. "Look. A friend sent me to offer you a job."

"I don't have any friends," Jake said, then added muttering beneath his breath, "and I'm not fit for any jobs."

"You're fit for the job he's got in mind," the man said. "Look, Cog, the only easy day was yesterday. Are you a SEAL or not?"

Cog.

Only the men he'd fought with side by side had called him Cog.

A frown pulled his brow low as he leaned forward in his chair. "Anyone can look up the SEAL motto. How do I know you're the real deal?" Jake had to admit he was curious now.

"You have to trust me." The man chuckled. "It's not like us Deltas have tridents tattooed on our foreheads like you Navy SEALs. My honor was forged in battle, just like yours."

Despite himself, Jake's lips twitched. No, they didn't have tridents, the symbol of their trade, drawn in indelible ink on their foreheads. But it was etched into their hearts. The grueling training they'd survived had made them proud to wear the symbol of the Navy SEAL and even prouder to fight as a team alongside the Delta Force operatives.

"Who sent you?" Jake asked.

"Hank Patterson," the voice said and waited.

A flood of memories washed over Jake. Hank had been his mentor when he'd come on board, fresh from BUD/S training. He hadn't hazed him as the others on the team had. He'd taken Jake beneath his wing and taught him everything he knew that would help him in the many missions to come. Many of Hank's techniques had kept Jake alive on more than one occasion. He owed the man his life.

"Why didn't Hank come himself?" Jake asked.

"He and his wife have a new baby. You might not be aware that his wife is a famous actress. She's going on set in a few days, and Hank has diaper duty."

"Hank? Diaper duty?" Jake shook his head. The alcohol in his system made his vision blur. "Doesn't sound like Hank."

"Well, it is. Will you open the door so we can discuss his proposition?"

Jake glanced around the pathetic excuse of an apartment and shook his head. "No. But I'll come out in a minute. You can buy me a drink, and we can talk."

"Good," the man said. "Anything to get out of this hallway. Your neighbors are giving me threatening looks."

Jake reached for his prosthesis, pulled up his pantleg, donned the inner sleeve, slipped his stump into position and pulled the outer sleeve over his thigh. He slid his good foot into a shoe and pushed to a standing position, swaying slightly.

He smelled like dirty clothes and alcohol. But he'd

be damned if he let Hank's emissary into the apartment to see how low Jake Cogburn had sunk.

Lifting his shirt up to his nose, he grimaced. Then he yanked it over his head, slung it across the room and reached into the duffel bag in the corner for another T-shirt.

The sniff test had him flinging that shirt across the room to land with the other in a heap on the floor. Two shirts later, he settled on a black Led Zeppelin T-shirt that had been a gift from one of his buddies on his last SEAL team. The man had been a fan of one of the biggest bands of the seventies, a time way before he'd been born.

Running a hand through his hair, he shoved his socked-foot and his prosthetic foot into a pair of boots and finally opened the door.

The man on the other side leaned against the opposite wall in the hallway. He pushed away from the wall and held out his hand. "Jake Cogburn, I'm Joseph Kuntz. My friends call me Kujo."

Jake gave the man a narrow-eyed glare but took the hand. "What kind of job does Hank have in mind. Not that I'm interested." He shook the hand and let go quickly.

"He's started a business up in Montana and wants to open up a branch here in Colorado." Kujo ran his glance over Jake.

Jake's shoulders automatically squared. "And?"

"And he wants you to head it up."

Jake laughed out loud. "Hank wants this broken-down SEAL to head up an office?"

Kujo nodded. "He does."

"Why don't *you* do it?"

"I have a pregnant wife back in Montana. I only have a few weeks to help you lay the groundwork. Then I have to get back."

His head shaking back and forth, Jake stared at the man as if he'd lost his mind. "What the hell kind of business can a one-legged ex-SEAL manage? Does he even know me?"

"He said he mentored you as a newbie SEAL a long time back. He knows your service record and thinks you would make the perfect man to lead the new branch." Kujo crossed his arms over his chest. "He has confidence that you have the skills needed to do the job. And there's no such thing as an ex-SEAL. Once a SEAL, always a SEAL."

Jake nodded. The man was right. "He knew me back then. But does he know me now?" Jake touched the thigh of his injured leg.

Kujo nodded. "He knows about your circumstances, and he's still certain you're the one to do the job."

Jake shook his head. "What exactly will this branch of his business sell?"

"We're a service organization. We provide security and unique skills to our clients to protect them and/or take care of situations law enforcement or the military might not be in a position to assist with."

"Vigilantes?" Kujo held up his hands. "No thanks."

"Not vigilantes," Kujo said. "More a security service for those in need of highly trained special ops folks who know how to handle a gun and run a tactical mission."

"Again," Jake said, "sounds like vigilantes. No thanks. Besides, I'm not fit to fight. The Navy told me so." He turned to go back into his apartment and find another whiskey glass.

Kujo stepped between him and the door. "Can you fire a weapon?"

Jake shrugged. "Sure. Nothing wrong with my hands and arms. But I can't run, jump and maneuver the way I used to before..." He tipped his chin toward his prosthesis.

"You still have a brain. You can compensate," Kujo raised his eyebrows. "Do you have a job?"

Jake's chest tightened. "No."

Kujo's chin lifted a fraction. "Then, what do you have to lose?" He stood with his shoulders back, his head held high—the way Jake used to stand.

What did he have to lose? He'd lost everything that had been important to him. He couldn't sink any lower. His brows furrowing, he stared into Kujo's open, friendly face and then shrugged. "I have nothing to lose."

Kujo nodded. "Trust me. I've been there. Hank Patterson brought me out of the hell I'd sunk into. Life has only gotten better since."

"Well, you have both legs," Jake pointed out.

"And you have your hands and mind, one perfectly good leg and a prosthetic device you can get around on just fine from what I can see." He frowned. "Are you going to stand around bellyaching or come with me and start a new job I think you'll love."

"I'm not bellyaching," Jake grumbled.

"But you're wasting daylight, and I have another place I need to be before dark." Kujo stood back. "What's it to be?"

For a tense moment, Jake stood fast. After weeks of wallowing in the hovel of an apartment, getting out seemed more difficult than staying with the familiar.

"Why did Hank choose me?" he asked.

"Based on your past performance as a Navy SEAL, Hank thought you were the right person for the task he had in mind. He trusts you, your work and your integrity. The job won't always be easy…" Kujo grinned. "But the only easy day…"

"Yeah, yeah…was yesterday." Jake impatiently waved Kujo ahead of him. "I'm coming. But don't take that as a yes. I have yet to decide whether I want to work for Hank."

Kujo cocked an eyebrow. "You have a better job offer?"

Jake wanted to tell the man that he did, but he couldn't. "No."

"Fine. Come with me. We have another stop to make before we seal this deal and kick off this project." Kujo nodded toward the interior of the apartment. "Got a go bag?"

Jake glanced back. "Not since I left the service. Why?"

"We'll most likely stay the night where we're going. Maybe longer. Grab what you need for a couple of days."

Jake returned to his apartment, grabbed the duffel bag out of the bottom of the closet and stuffed a pair of jeans, socks, underwear, some T-shirts, a jacket and his shaving kit into it. He returned to his apartment entrance where Kujo waited.

The other man stepped outside and waited for Jake to follow.

Jake carried his bag through the door and pulled it closed behind him. "Where are we going?"

"To a ranch."

His feet coming to an immediate halt, Jake shook his head. "Why are we going to a ranch? You didn't say anything about a ranch."

Kujo drew in a deep breath and let it go slowly, as if he was holding back his own impatience. "Bear with me. I'll fill you in when we get there. Just suffice it to say, your job will be important to someone."

"Who?"

Kujo grinned. "Whoever needs you most."

"That's kind of vague, if you ask me."

"It's the nature of the work," Kujo said.

"Just what exactly does this job entail?" Jake asked.

"Don't worry." Kujo led the way down the stairs of

the apartment complex and out to a shiny, black SUV. "I fully intend to brief you on your position and the nature of Hank's organization. But first, I'd like to get out of here and up into the mountains."

Jake climbed into the SUV, silently cursing his prosthetic when it banged against the door. Once in his seat, he buckled his seatbelt, wondering what the hell he was doing and when the hell he'd get that drink Kujo promised. Thankfully, he hadn't committed to anything, which was his only saving grace. What kind of job could Hank have in mind for a one-legged, former Navy SEAL?

CHAPTER 2

"RJ? YOU OUT BACK AGAIN?" a voice like rocks rattling in a bucket called out.

Striker took up a protective stance. The Military Working Dog RJ had adopted a month before was still learning how to live a non-working life. He stood his ground and growled deep in his throat.

RJ, or as her father had documented on her birth certificate, Rucker Juliet Tate, patted the Belgian Malinois's head. "It's okay," she murmured. "It's just Gunny." Then she tossed the heavy bag of trash into the bin and turned toward the back door of Gunny's Watering Hole, the bar just outside of town and conveniently situated at their home, the Lost Valley Ranch. "Yes, sir," she replied. "Just emptying the trash."

Her father, former Marine Gunnery Sergeant Daniel Tate—Gunny to anyone who knew him—stepped out the back door and pushed his straw cowboy hat back on his head. "You got plans for this evening?"

She snorted. "Do I ever have plans on a Monday night?"

Her father's lips twisted. "No. But I keep hoping you will."

"And leave you to run this place and the ranch by yourself?" She shook her head and gave him a gentle smile.

"I can manage." Gunny shook his head. "Though, why I thought a dude ranch and a bar were good ideas, I'll never know."

"You needed something to do in your retirement, and you know it." She planted her fists on her hips. "What's up?"

"I think our prospects," he said with a twisted grin.

RJ's eyes narrowed. "What do you mean *our prospects?*"

"Got a call from an old friend the other day. He wants to use our place as a base for a business he wants to run here in Colorado."

RJ's frown deepened. "He wants to buy us out?"

"No," Gunny said. "He just wants to rent space."

"Space? As in the barn or the lodge?"

"Some of both." Gunny held up his hands. "He wants us to continue our own operation, as is, but he needs a location for his business. And you know how hard it is to make money with this dude ranch."

"No kidding. The bar is the only thing keeping us going through the winter months."

Her father nodded. "And even then, only when we don't have heavy snows."

The wheels in RJs head spun. "How much is he willing to pay in rent?"

Gunny named a figure.

RJ whistled. "What kind of business is he running? Drugs?"

"We'll find out soon. Two of his guys are on their way out. I don't know whether to clean or just let them see this place, as is."

RJ shook her head. "Gunny, this place is clean. Any cleaner, and people won't think it's a dude ranch or a bar." She wiped her hands on the sides of her jeans. "When will they be here?"

"Any minute. I need to set aside a couple of rooms in the lodge for them as well. I'm not sure if they're only visiting or going to stay the night."

"Seriously, Gunny? And you're just now telling me?"

He lifted one shoulder. "I wasn't sure when they'd arrive until I got the call a little while ago."

RJ lifted her chin. "I don't care how much money they offer...if their business isn't legit, we don't want anything to do with it. We've worked too hard on this place to have it confiscated by the DEA, FBI or any other government organization."

Her father laughed. "If I know Hank Patterson, it's legit. He's one of the finest Navy SEALs I've ever had the pleasure to know. I'd bet my life that he's on the up and up."

RJ crossed her arms over her chest. "Still, I want to hear them out before we commit in writing."

"Fair enough." Her father tipped his head toward her shirt. "You might want to change into a clean shirt. That one has mustard on it."

RJ glanced down at the shirt she'd been wearing through the bar's lunch crowd. Like her father indicated, she had a bright yellow smear of mustard across her left breast. "This is your place. I don't need to impress them."

Her father's chin lifted, and he stared down his nose at her in the way he reserved for Marine recruits. The man didn't have to say a word. That look was more than enough.

"Yes, sir," she said and popped a mock salute. "I'll change, right away." She turned away from the back of the bar and headed for the lodge where she and her father lived and worked the dude ranching operations during the day. The bar operated at lunch and later.

"You might also comb your hair," Gunny called out after her. "And hurry. They'll be here in less than fifteen minutes. I'll need you to man the bar while we talk."

RJ picked up her pace, walking fast to reach the lodge. She didn't care if she had mustard on her shirt. To her, it was a proud sign of the fact that she'd been working hard. If the men coming to see her father didn't see it the same way, they didn't need their money.

Well, they really did.

She still wasn't convinced their business was on the legal side. Then again, the income from renting them space on the Lost Valley Ranch might help cover their expenses for the year.

RJ crossed her fingers as she took the steps up to her room inside the lodge, two at a time, Striker on her heels. Once she'd closed and locked the door behind herself and Striker, she pulled the blue chambray shirt from where it was tucked into the waistband of her jeans, unbuttoned a few buttons and yanked it over her head, flinging it into the wicker clothes basket she kept in a corner. Even in her haste, she couldn't leave dirty clothing lying on the floor.

Her father, being the Marine gunnery sergeant he'd been, had raised her to run a tight ship. She was almost as OCD about cleanliness as he was.

Despite Gunny's discipline and taciturn manner, he was a softy to the core and loved RJ with all his heart.

The man had raised her from her beginning, after her mother had died in childbirth, sacrificing much of his career in the Marines to provide a safe and loving home for her. He'd deployed a couple of times when she'd been little. When they were stationed at Coronado, he'd met a young Navy SEAL who'd made a big impression on the older Marine.

RJ guessed that young Navy SEAL had been Hank

Patterson, the one calling in a favor and, by doing so, could actually help Gunny and RJ in a huge way.

Gunny had been pouring over the books just a week ago, wondering how they would pay the mortgage and utilities for the place. The winter had been harsh, not allowing many to venture out to the bar.

The previous summer, a nearby forest fire had cut their business in half. Fortunately, rain had come to tamp down the flames before the fire reached the Lost Valley Ranch.

RJ had seriously considered looking for a job in Colorado Springs to help supplement the Lost Valley Ranch coffers.

Having the rental income from Hank's business could potentially save them from having to put the ranch up for sale.

RJ rummaged through her closet for a clean shirt. Her hands skimmed over several more of the same well-worn, blue chambray shirts she preferred to wear while both mucking the stalls and bartending at Gunny's Watering Hole. She'd found it safer than dressing all girlie. At least she wasn't harassed by the guests of the ranch or the bar patrons when she looked like a ranch hand or just one of the guys.

And she kept her hair pulled back in a tight ponytail. On several occasions, she'd threatened to cut her long wavy blond hair, but her father talked her out of it every time.

"Your mother wore her hair long, and you're the spitting image of Grace." He'd looked so sad and nostalgic RJ couldn't go through with it. She compromised by pulling it back into a tight ponytail or a knot at the nape of her neck, and then wearing a cowboy hat when she was outside.

Her hand swept past the faded shirts to the one dress she owned, a simple black dress she'd worn once to a funeral.

She shook her head and moved past it to the powder-blue rib-knit, short-sleeved sweater her friend JoJo had given to her as a birthday present. She'd worn it to the last outdoor dance the city of Fool's Gold had set up in City Park.

JoJo had insisted RJ go with her to provide safety in numbers. Two lone females were better than one.

RJ hadn't wanted to go, but JoJo had insisted, dragging her along. And she'd actually danced with a couple of the local men. Though Gunny hadn't taught her much about being a girl, he'd been sure to teach her how to two-step.

At the time, RJ hadn't understood the importance of knowing her way around a dance floor. Thankfully, her father had taught her how to dance, and she was able to keep up even with the best dancers. It had been the first time since she'd left college that she'd dared to do anything that wasn't related to the ranch or the bar.

Gunny had tried to get her to go out with friends, but she'd let her friends from high school and college slide out of her life. They had all moved on, gotten married and had children. The drive out to the ranch was too far for most to consider, even if she'd invited them.

And RJ didn't have time to drive into Colorado Springs. Between her and her father, they had more than enough work to do for four or five people.

RJ pulled the blue sweater over her head, slipped out of her work boots and faded jeans and reached for a less faded pair of jeans. Her hand paused in mid-air as she spotted the jean skirt JoJo had given her along with the sweater.

On impulse, she stepped into the skirt, pulled it up over her hips and zipped the front. It fit the curve of her hips perfectly. JoJo would be glad to see her finally wear it. And her friend would see it when she came in to help wait on tables at the bar in… RJ glanced down at her watch.

Damn, she'd been gone for ten minutes. The bar was due to open now. If the two men had shown up already, her father wouldn't have time to meet with them. JoJo wouldn't get there for another thirty minutes.

Standing in her socks, she glanced at the bottom of her closet. She owned two pairs of boots, tennis shoes and a pair of low-heeled black shoes she'd worn with the black dress to the funeral.

With a sigh, she pulled on her best cowboy boots and grabbed her brush from the top of her dresser.

One glance in the mirror made her yelp.

Striker whimpered and nuzzled her hand.

"Sorry. I forget you're a little skittish with sudden

noises." She rubbed a hand over his head. "It's okay. Well, you're okay, but my hair looks like something the cat dragged in."

Striker whimpered again.

"Don't like cats?" RJ asked. "Shhh. Don't tell Tiger he's a cat. He's already a freeloader out in the barn. He might get a complex if other cats find out he's a terrible mouser."

Several thick strands of her silky hair had slipped out of the elastic band. With no time to spare, she pulled the band free, swiped at the tangles with the brush and called it done.

RJ darted down the stairs. Striker took the stairs a bit slower, not too bothered by the fact he had only three legs to balance on. RJ burst out of the lodge, passing the older couple who were regulars, coming out to stay with them every summer for the past five years. "Hello, Mr. and Mrs. Pendergast."

Mrs. Pendergast's eyebrows rose up her forehead. "RJ?"

RJ slowed so fast Striker ran into the backs of her legs. "Sorry, I can't stop and chat. Gotta work the bar tonight."

Mr. Pendergast gave her a thumbs up. "Looking good, RJ."

"Yes, you are," Mrs. Pendergast said. "That color suits you, as does the skirt. And I like your hair down."

Unused to compliments, RJ pushed a hand through her hair. "Thank you."

Mrs. Pendergast touched her arm. "You're a beautiful young woman, RJ. You should be proud."

RJ shook her head. "My mother was beautiful. I take after my father."

"No matter who you take after, you're lovely," Mr. Pendergast said. "We'll be by after our afternoon constitutional."

"See ya then," RJ said and scooted to the bar, Striker following. They entered through the front door.

She stood for a moment, letting her vision adjust to the dim lighting in the bar after being out in the afternoon sunshine.

A hand gripped her arm and dragged her through the room. "RJ, where have you been, Chica?" JoJo demanded. Josephina Angelica Barrera-Rodriguez stood all of five feet tall in her shoes. She made up for her small stature in fierceness. When she got mad or excited, her Latina heritage came out in a flurry of Spanish. "Your father is busy with those men, and I need some drink orders filled."

"On it," RJ said, hurrying toward the bar. She walked around to the other side and glanced across at her friend. "What do you need?"

JoJo grinned. "I need to know what the occasion is that got you into a skirt."

Her face heating, RJ grabbed a rag and swiped at the counter. "Gunny told me to wear something clean."

"And that's all you had?" JoJo laughed.

Her cheeks burning hotter, RJ glanced up. "I didn't say that. And this outfit is really nice. If I didn't say it already, thank you."

JoJo cursed in Spanish. "*De nada*. But I wasn't looking for gratitude. Not that it's any of my business, I just want to know what's going on." She jerked her head toward the back door. "For starters, who were the two big guys with Gunny. Do I need to call in some of my cousins to protect the old man?"

RJ frowned. "Did they look like they'd hurt him?" She started for the rear exit.

"No, really, RJ, it's okay," JoJo said.

RJ turned back to her friend. "Are you sure?"

The petite Hispanic woman nodded her dark head. "They shook hands and smiled when they came into the bar." Her brow wrinkled. "At least, one of them did. And he was the one doing all the talking."

"Maybe I need to see for myself." Again, she started to turn.

"I'm sure they're all right."

A man shouted from the far corner of the barroom. "Hey, JoJo, you gonna bring us our drinks, or do we have to come get them?"

JoJo pulled a page off her order book and slapped it on the counter. "That's our cue. We have some thirsty customers tonight. You'd better get cracking. Gunny is a grown man. He can handle those two guys."

"Yeah, but I wanted to hear what they were saying," she grumbled as she filled the order, disappointed that they hadn't included her in their conversation.

"I'm sure he'll fill you in when all is said and done." JoJo lifted the heavy tray of drinks. "Gunny tells you everything."

"Not everything," RJ muttered. "He didn't tell me he'd had a call from this Hank person who sent those goons out here."

JoJo didn't hear her words. She was already halfway across the floor to deliver drinks to the thirsty patrons of the Watering Hole.

It was just as well RJ wasn't included in the conversation among the three men. If they were people her father had served with in the military, he'd have more in common with them than she would.

Again, she wished she'd been accepted into the Army when she and JoJo had gone through the Military Entry Processing Station right after high school.

While JoJo sailed through with no problems, RJ had been medically screened and disqualified for a heart murmur she'd never known she had.

Their plans to see the world and serve their country together had all been crushed. JoJo had to go on without her.

RJ had remained in Colorado with her father.

Gunny had sunk his entire life savings into buying the Lost Valley Ranch. He and RJ spent the next ten years fixing it up, repairing fences and running cattle. When the cattle wasn't enough to keep up with the mortgage payments, they'd opened up the bar and the ranch to tourists eager to get a taste of high mountain living.

JoJo returned with empty mugs and bottles.

RJ quickly cleared her tray and filled it again. As she walked away with the filled tray, RJ studied her friend.

JoJo had served eight years in the Army and had come back a different person. Someone or something had hurt her while she'd been on active duty. The dark circles beneath her eyes reflected a lingering sadness or inability to sleep.

RJ couldn't get her to talk about it. JoJo said she didn't want RJ to get involved.

Being her best friend, RJ hadn't been able to stand back and do nothing. She'd introduced JoJo to another friend, Emily Strayhorn, who happened to be a therapist and a stray Gunny had taken in during hard times and let live at the ranch until she'd completed her degree and the hours required to attain her certification.

"Hey, JoJo." RJ took the order sheet from JoJo on her next pass back to the bar. "How have your sessions with Emily been going?"

JoJo shrugged. "Okay, I guess. She's just someone to talk to when I'm feeling down."

"You know you can talk to me, too."

JoJo reached a hand across the bar and touched RJ's arm. "I know. And I appreciate your concern. But I've known you most of my life. Strange as it seems, I feel more comfortable talking to someone I don't really know."

"I guess I get that." RJ's lips twisted. "As long as you know I'd do anything for you. I've got your back." On a softer tone, she added, "Wish I could have been with you in the Army."

JoJo's jaw hardened, and the shadows deepened in her eyes. "I'm glad you weren't."

Before RJ could dig deeper into JoJo's comment, a customer shouted, "JoJo! Where's my drink?"

"Duty calls." JoJo grabbed the tray of drinks and hurried to deliver.

RJ glanced at her watch. She'd been tending bar for two hours and still no sign of Gunny and the two men who'd left with him. What could be taking them so long? The lodge, barn and bar weren't that big. Surely, there wasn't that much to talk about? You want to rent space? How much? Hell, they could have the entire ranch for what Hank Patterson was willing to pay. Only thing Gunny needed to do was lock them into a contract for no less than a year.

If they could continue to run their dude ranch operations and the bar at the same time, it would be icing on the cake.

RJ lifted a bottle from the back shelf.

"RJ?" JoJo called out.

Bottle in hand, RJ turned quickly. The bottle hit the countertop at just the right angle and broke, sending shards of glass and a spray of alcohol all over the floor. "Damn!"

"Are you all right?" JoJo appeared on the other side of the counter.

"I'm fine. I just wasted half a bottle of our best tequila."

"I'm sorry. I shouldn't have yelled out your name." JoJo sighed. "Take it out of my paycheck. I insist."

RJ frowned. "No way. I was the clumsy one. Think you can hold off the thirsty camels while I clean up this mess?"

"I've got this." JoJo grabbed a couple bowls of pretzels from the counter and spun toward a table where a pale-faced, lone man sat nursing a glass of whiskey.

RJ bent and gingerly picked up the largest shards of the bottle and dumped them into a waste basket. When she had all the big pieces of glass cleaned up, she hurried to the back supply room for the items she'd need to complete the cleanup. If she left the tequila on the floor, it would be slippery for a while and then turn sticky. Not an option, either way.

Gunny kept the bar area clean. He expected the same from her. And potential customers didn't need to see the mess.

When she started for the back rooms, Striker rose from where he'd been sleeping on a padded dog bed behind the bar.

"No, Striker," she said. "Stay."

The Malinois whimpered.

"I'll be right back." She didn't want the dog to cross over the tequila mess and broken glass. His paws could be cut in the process. "Stay," she repeated and left him behind the bar while she headed for the back rooms.

In the supply closet, she found the broom, dustpan and mop bucket but no mop. Then she remembered she'd left it out on the back porch to dry the night before.

RJ stepped through the rear door and reached for the mop. Darkness had settled over the bar and ranch. The single yellow light glowing over the back porch lit her way. A sound startled her and made her turn toward the large trash container.

A shadowy form shifted back and forth in the darkness. After a second, RJ recognized it as two men in a scuffle. Nothing unusual for a Saturday night in the mountains. But she didn't want it to reflect badly on the Watering Hole or the Lost Valley Ranch when Gunny was attempting to sell the new guys on renting a quiet place in the country.

Punches flew between them, one guy staggering backward to hit the steel corner of the trash bin with a resounding thud. Then he slid to the ground. The other guy approached him with his arm cocked, his hand balled into a fist. He was going to hit the man while he was obviously down.

"Hey!" RJ called out as she flew off the porch and raced toward the last man standing. "Leave him alone!"

The guy spun and faced her, a ski mask covering his face.

The cold hand of dread clenched around RJ's chest. This wasn't a typical barfight. A guy wearing a ski mask had something to hide.

Anger surged through RJ, and she lost her grip on caution. Charging forward, she reached for the man's ski mask.

Before he could knock her hand away, she sank her fingers into the black knit threads and tugged it free of his head.

At the same time, a fist came out and crashed into her temple, knocking her backward.

RJ lost her balance and fell flat on her back, her hard landing knocking the wind from her lungs.

Shocked by the fall, she couldn't move for several seconds and could only see the stars swirling around her head.

A dark shadow fell over her, and her attacker reached down, grabbed the ski mask from her hands and slipped it over his head and face. Then he smashed his palm over RJ's mouth and nose, leaned his body over hers and trapped her arms and legs with his weight.

RJ, already breathless from her fall, couldn't draw in air. She fought with all her might, but the man was heavier and had the advantage.

Her vision, already compromised by her fall, blurred further, the gray turning to black around the edges until her strength waned and fight seeped out of her limbs. With no air to recharge her brain and muscles, she went limp, fading into a black abyss.

Suddenly, the weight jerked off her.

In the darkness, as if from far away, she heard scuffling and several thumping sounds and grunts.

RJ could do nothing. Her hearing seemed to return, but she wasn't really there. It was as if she'd left her body and hovered over the scene in a haze of gloom.

Footsteps crunched in the gravel, and someone was speaking.

"Hey, lady," a deep resonant voice called out as if at the end of a long tunnel.

RJ couldn't answer, couldn't move, couldn't open her eyes.

Then something soft and warm covered her lips. Fuzz tickled the skin on her cheek. If she could feel that, she wasn't dead, was she?

Air filled her mouth and pushed down her throat into her lungs. It left as quickly as it came but more followed. Two, three, four times, air pushed into her.

The haze of darkness drifted away. Soft, yellow light peeked between her eyelids.

People were talking. A little closer this time.

"What the hell?" a man's familiar voice sounded near her. "RJ? RJ, baby?"

Gunny. She thought she spoke it, but no sound came from her mouth. Her lips were still covered, and air was being forced into her lungs.

As the fog cleared in her mind, her body took over. Tingling began in her fingers and toes and spread up her arms and legs. Then her lungs engaged, and she gasped.

"There you are," that deep resonant voice sounded, warm breath feathering across her cheek.

RJ's eyes fluttered open, and she stared up at the dark silhouette of a man with a heavy beard and dark eyes.

"RJ? Oh, baby, are you okay?" her father called out.

"I…think…so," she said, suddenly aware of hands on her arms. Warm, large hands.

When she tried to sit up, those hands held her back. "Lie still. We don't know if you have other injuries we can't see."

"Injuries?" RJ said, her mind returning function but not with memories intact. "Why….what…?" She stared at the man holding her arms. "Who are you?"

"Jake," he said. "And you are?"

"Rucker Juliet Tate," she whispered automatically. "You can call me RJ."

He gave her a hint of a smile. "RJ. Nice to meet you." Then he turned to address someone nearby. "Kujo, did you check the other guy?"

Another unfamiliar voice answered. "Too late for him. He's dead."

Gunny's face appeared beside Jake's. "Thank goodness you were here, or my baby girl would be the same." His hand touched Jake's shoulder as he stared into RJ's eyes. "What happened?"

RJ lay on the hard ground, gravel digging into her back, and shook her head. "I'm not sure."

"I just put in a call to 911," the other man said. "An ambulance is on its way."

RJ moved her arms and legs, one by one, checking for any abnormalities. When she found none, she tried again to sit up.

Jake's hands held her down. "You could have a spinal injury. Moving could make it worse."

She frowned. "Let me up. I'm okay. I don't need an ambulance." She reached up and shoved his hands aside.

Jake pushed to his feet, favoring one leg. He swayed a bit before he straightened and held out a hand to her. "If you're sure..."

She didn't want to accept his help, but still didn't feel completely in control of her own body. Laying her hand in his, she let him help her to her feet.

Jake pulled with enough force, she came off the ground and pitched forward into his chest.

His arms rose around her, his hands finding her hips, steadying her against him.

He took an awkward step backward, again, favoring his left leg.

RJ stood with her hands pressed to his chest, feeling the hard muscles beneath her fingertips, glad for his strength when she felt like a bowl of limp noodles.

Since he and his friend were with Gunny, they

had to be the men who'd come to check out Lost Valley Ranch as a potential business location.

And she'd just made a great first impression by failing to keep a customer alive and getting knocked out herself.

Not that he was a stellar representative of a businessman. He wore a Led Zeppelin T-shirt, and his hair needed to be cut and his beard trimmed.

All that didn't matter. The man had saved her life. Her lips tingled from where his had been, forcing air into her lungs.

She looked past the thick beard, the unkempt hair and the rocker T-shirt, up into Jake's dark eyes. They held shadows of their own. Shadows that made RJ wonder at their cause.

She shook herself, bringing her mind back to what really mattered. She owed this man her life. "Thank you for saving me."

CHAPTER 3

JAKE GRUNTED A RESPONSE. He hadn't asked to be the one to save this woman in the soft sweater and short skirt. He'd just happened to want another beer and had excused himself from the meeting he and Kujo had been having in the lodge to get a drink from the bar.

Since he'd left the bar through the back door, he'd assumed it was okay to reenter from that direction.

He hadn't anticipated rescuing a woman who was clearly being smothered to death. But he was glad he'd been there. Otherwise, there would've been two bodies to clean up instead of one. And it would've been a shame if RJ hadn't survived.

"You're welcome," he said.

RJ glanced down at the man lying on the ground, his head at an awkward angle, his face white in the starlight. "Who was he?"

"I'm not sure," Gunny said. "He's not a regular. Not one from around Fool's Gold that I know."

RJ shook her head as if in an attempt to clear the remaining fog. The man's face swam into her memory. "He was in the bar earlier, sitting alone at one of the tables JoJo was waiting on."

As if on cue, a petite woman flew out the back door and raced down the porch steps, followed by a large dog.

"RJ? Oh, sweet Jesus…RJ?" The dark-haired woman came to an abrupt halt behind the woman leaning against Jake's chest. "Are you all right? I turn my back for a moment, and you're gone." The petite woman looked up at Jake, her brow dipping. "Is this man hurting you? Because if he is…" She raised her fists and snarled at him.

The dog leaned against RJ's leg and whined.

RJ chuckled, her hand going to the animal's head as she addressed the other woman. "No, JoJo. This man saved me." She pushed away from his chest and turned toward the smaller woman. "I'm okay. See?"

"What happened out here?" JoJo asked, her gaze going to Gunny and Kujo, and then finally, to the man on the ground. A gasp escaped her. "Is he…?"

"Dead?" Kujo answered. "Yes."

The woman's eyes rounded, and she touched RJ's arm. "Did you…kill him? Because if you did, I'm sure he had it coming."

RJ pulled JoJo into her arms and hugged her tightly. "No. I didn't kill him. Someone else did."

"And then proceeded to try to kill your friend," Jake added. "Do you know this man?" he asked JoJo.

She shook her head. "No. Tonight was the first time I've seen him in the bar."

"Did he close out his tab with a credit card?" Gunny asked.

Again, JoJo shook her head. "No. He paid cash. And left a hefty tip." Her hand went to the pocket of her jeans, and she glanced toward Gunny. "He asked to talk to Mr. Tate. I told him you were in a meeting." Her brow furrowed. "Should I have come to get you?"

Gunny shook his head. "No. You were busy, and I was in a meeting."

"JoJo," RJ touched the small woman's shoulder, "This man's death is not your fault. You didn't kill him. The man in the ski mask did." She pulled her friend into a hug and held her close.

Jake's chest warmed at how much the people of Lost Valley Ranch and the Watering Hole cared for each other. It reminded him of his SEAL team and the brotherhood they'd shared through good times and more challenging events.

Gunny squatted beside the dead man and felt in his pockets, unearthing a leather wallet. He straightened and carried it over to the light. Gunny located the man's driver's license. "Robert Henderson. And he lives in Colorado Springs." The old Marine rummaged through the rest of the wallet and pulled out a business card. "He's a broker for a real estate company in the springs."

"Wonder what brought him out this far," RJ said.

"In real estate, he could show properties throughout Colorado Springs as well as up here in Fool's Gold," Gunny said. "Maybe he was showing a property earlier and stopped in the bar for a drink before heading back to the springs."

"That's likely," RJ said. "But who would want to hurt him? The man who attacked us was wearing a ski mask." A frown settled on her brow. She pinched the bridge of her nose and closed her eyes. "I pulled his mask off."

"Did you get a look at the man's face?" Kujo asked.

RJ's hand rose to her temple where a bruise was forming. She sighed and opened her eyes. "No. He hit me before I could get a look at his face. Then he was smothering me, and I…can't remember much until I came to." Her gaze went to Jake's. "I don't suppose you saw his face?"

Jake's jaw tightened. "He was wearing the ski mask when I pulled him off you. I would've gone after him, but you weren't breathing. I couldn't leave you."

"You did the right thing," Gunny said. "RJ's life was more important than catching the killer. The authorities will find him."

Sirens sounded in the distance.

"You realize the attacker committed a murder and almost got away with another, right?" Kujo nodded toward RJ. "If he thinks she can identify him, he might come back."

Gunny's eyes narrowed. "You think he might come back after RJ?"

Kujo shrugged. "She is potentially the only witness to this crime, who might have seen his face." His gaze captured RJ's. "You might still be in danger."

"This is insane," RJ said, shoving a hand through her tangled hair. "We haven't had this kind of crime in or around Fool's Gold, much less, the Lost Valley Ranch, since I've been here."

"She's right," Gunny said. "Fool's Gold is a sleepy little town. The only crime we see is around the casino on the other end of town and an occasional barroom fight when the guys have a little too much to drink."

"And Gunny makes sure they get home, driving them himself when they can't find someone sober to do the job," RJ added.

"Who would want to kill a stranger way out here?" JoJo murmured, her gaze on the dead man lying against the trash bin.

"Guess we'll find out," Gunny said as a Teller County Sheriff's SUV pulled to a halt beside the bar. An ambulance followed right behind the sheriff's vehicle. Red and white strobe lights lit up the area as the sirens faded. The first responders jumped down and hurried toward the dead man.

Gunny met the sheriff's deputy as he stepped out of his vehicle.

"What have we got here, Gunny?" the deputy asked.

"One dead, and my daughter was attacked and almost killed," Gunny responded.

The deputy turned to Jake and Kujo. "And these men are?"

Gunny stepped forward. "Deputy Ray Gathright, this is Joseph Kuntz and Jake Cogburn, my business associates."

Deputy Gathright held out a hand to Kujo. "Mr. Kuntz. Pleasure."

"You can call me Kujo."

The deputy's brow wrinkled. "Isn't that the name of a rabid dog, or something, from a movie?"

Kujo chuckled. "It is. Different spelling. The name came about during Basic Combat Training. Last name Kuntz. First name Joseph. One of the DI's shortened it to Kujo, and it stuck."

"Kujo, it is." The deputy shook his hand and turned to shake Jake's. "Business associates?"

Kujo nodded. "We're renting space at the Lost Valley Ranch."

"Tourists?"

A smile tweaked the corners of Kujo's mouth. "Not exactly. I used to live in Colorado. But this will be Cog—Jake's—territory when I leave to return home."

"And home is?" Gathright asked.

"Montana," Kujo answered.

Gathright cocked an eyebrow. "I'll need you two to hang around. Since this appears to be a homicide, the state police will want to get involved with the investigation. I'm sure they'll want to ask you a few questions."

"Ray," RJ spoke up, "Mr. Cogburn didn't kill that man. He kept the killer from killing me."

"I understand," the deputy said. "We'll still need statements from Mr. Cogburn and Mr. Kuntz. It would be best if they stuck around."

Patrons from inside the bar came out and gathered around, trying to see what was happening and talking among themselves.

Deputy Gathright turned to the crowd. "I'll need everyone to stick around until I can gather names and statements."

A few of the men grumbled, but they didn't try to leave.

The deputy cordoned off the area around the dead man while JoJo and RJ herded the bar patrons back into the building with a promise of coffee on the house.

Thirty minutes later, the state police crime investigation unit arrived and went about dusting for latent prints, taking pictures and questioning the patrons regarding what they might have seen or heard in the building or in the parking lot.

No one had seen anything, except for Gunny's daughter. And she couldn't remember much.

The killer had gotten away without being identified. Which meant he was still out there. And if he was still out there, he could come back for RJ to make sure she didn't remember anything she might have seen when his mask was off.

Not that Gunny's daughter was his responsibility, but after bringing her back to life, Jake felt a certain need to keep her alive.

The fact that her lips had been soft, and her breath smelled like mint didn't have anything to do with his sudden streak of protectiveness. He didn't want her to be the victim of a killer who didn't think twice about smothering an innocent woman.

RJ and JoJo went inside to take care of the people the deputy had asked to stick around. With RJ out of his sight, Jake grew twitchy. He wanted to follow her.

As the authorities took over and worked the crime scene, Gunny gestured toward the bar. "Could I offer you men something to drink?"

"Yes," Jake answered, perhaps too quickly. He didn't want the drink so much as to see that RJ was okay.

Kujo nodded. "I could use a cup of coffee."

"We've got that. Coffee is always free for the designated drivers at the Watering Hole." Gunny led the way into the bar.

The tension in Jake's shoulders didn't relax until he saw RJ behind the bar, smiling at a customer while she poured a steaming cup of coffee.

Her smile lit the dim interior of the bar, and her laughter touched something inside Jake. How could she laugh after nearly being smothered to death? Obviously, Gunny had raised his daughter to be resilient. She hadn't fallen apart when she'd come to. She hadn't cried or screamed in hysterics like some women might in similar circumstances.

Rucker Juliet Tate had taken it all in and gotten back up on her feet. Now, she helped others when she should've let the emergency medical technicians look her over. She could have a concussion from the blow she'd taken to the head.

Hell, Jake could learn a thing or two from her. Like, don't take the knocks lying down. Get up and get back to work.

His hand went to his leg.

No, she hadn't lost a limb. But she'd almost lost her life. Yet, she wasn't crying about it.

Jake stepped up to the bar beside Kujo.

Gunny slipped behind the counter. "Jake, you want that beer you came out to get?"

Jake tipped his head toward RJ. "I'd rather have a cup of that coffee if there's any left."

"I'll have the same," Kujo seconded.

Gunny turned to his daughter. "RJ? You got a cup of Joe for Mr. Cogburn and Mr. Kuntz?"

"I do," she said and pulled two mugs from a shelf behind her and set them on the counter in front of Jake and Kujo. The Belgian Malinois that had followed her inside stayed right beside her, as if sensing she needed protection.

Jake felt a kinship to the dog. He, too, felt the need to stay close to the woman.

RJ poured steaming liquid into the mugs. "Sugar or cream?"

Kujo held up a hand. "None for me."

RJ cocked an eyebrow toward Jake. "You?"

"I like mine black."

"Can I get you anything else?" she asked. "I can make up some sandwiches, if you're hungry."

"I promised our guests a couple of steaks for dinner before everything went to hell," Gunny said. "If you tide yourselves over with pretzels, I'll come through with the steaks once the authorities are gone."

"Deal," Kujo said.

RJ filled a couple bowls with pretzels and set them on the counter in front of Kujo and Jake. "So, I take it you and my father came to some kind of agreement?"

Kujo nodded. "We did."

RJ wiped the counter with a clean rag. "How soon will you want to move your operations in?"

Gunny leaned close. "Immediately. They'll be staying in the lodge, starting tonight."

RJ's eyebrows rose.

"Is there a problem with that?" Jake asked.

"No," she said. "You don't waste time, do you?"

Kujo laughed. "No. We don't." He tipped his head toward JoJo, who'd arrived back at the bar with a tray filled with empty cups, mugs and bottles. "We'll fill you in over those steaks."

"Okay. Thanks," she said and hurried away to fill

drink orders for the petite waitress.

"Just so you know, I don't keep any secrets from my daughter," Gunny said. "She is every bit as involved in this ranch as I am, probably more so. And she can be trusted."

Jake tipped his coffee mug up and sipped the hot, fresh-brewed liquid that warmed a path all the way to his empty stomach.

Kujo's gaze followed RJ. "I have a feeling she might be our first assignment in Colorado."

Jake stiffened, his lips on the edge of his coffee cup and liquid flowing into his mouth.

Gunny frowned. "What do you mean?"

"The Brotherhood Protectors job is to protect those who need it." Kujo faced Gunny. "After what happened tonight, your daughter needs that protection." Kujo clapped a hand onto Jake's back. "And Jake's just the man to provide that protection."

Jake spewed hot coffee on the counter in front of him.

RJ HAD JUST TURNED in time to see Jake spit out the coffee he was drinking. She hurried over with a washcloth and wiped up the droplets. "Sorry, I meant to tell you it was hot."

"It's not that," Jake said, setting his mug on the bar.

"No?" RJ frowned. "Then what was it?"

Kujo laughed and pounded Jake's back again.

"Yeah, Jake, what was it?"

RJ glanced toward her father.

Gunny met her gaze. "They're right."

Getting the feeling she wasn't going to like what *they* were going to be right about, RJ fisted her hands and planted them on her hips. "About what?"

"You need protection," Gunny said in his Marine gunnery sergeant, no-nonsense tone.

RJ's eyebrow rose. "You think that guy will be back?"

Kujo, Gunny and Jake nodded as one.

"That doesn't mean he will be back," RJ reasoned. "If it makes you feel better, I have a forty caliber pistol I can carry around. I do have my conceal carry permit."

"That will only work if you know how to use it," Kujo sad. "Do you?"

Gunny snorted. "She's been shooting since she was four years old. My RJ is a better shot than her old man."

"You're not an old man," RJ said. "And yes, I know how to use it and the dozen other guns we have here on the ranch."

"Yeah, but you don't have someone covering your six," said the bearded man with the deep voice that melted every bone in her body. The guy who'd saved her life.

"I do a pretty good job of taking care of myself," RJ retorted, hating the way her body reacted to the way Jake's words melted into every pore of her skin.

No man had ever made her so aware of every nerve ending with just his voice.

Frankly, it frightened her.

After the Army had medically disqualified her, she'd tucked her tail between her legs and gone home to help her father run the ranch he'd just purchased. Not that she'd been any more qualified to run a ranch than she'd been to join the Army, but she'd refused to be defeated yet again. Her father hadn't raised a coward. He'd raised a young woman who could learn anything and fight her way through any challenge placed in her path.

RJ had searched the internet, read books and apprenticed on neighboring ranches to learn the ropes she'd need to know to keep the Lost Valley Ranch viable and productive. When ranching cattle at high altitude proved to be less profitable, she'd suggested renting out the ranch to tourists, inviting them to get a taste of ranch life, offering hiking, climbing, trail rides and ATV tours in the summer.

In the winter, they offered cross-country skiing and snowmobile tours. The lodge had been a big single-family home that had seen better days when Gunny had bought it. Between the two of them, they'd upgraded the electrical and plumbing systems, added a couple of bathrooms and updated the kitchen, flooring and paint.

All the renovations she'd done working side by side with her father had left little time for her to date. Yeah, she'd gone out with some friends. Back when she was in high school, she'd had sex with one of the boys she'd fancied herself in love with. After the first couple of times, they'd both realized they just weren't that into each other and had broke up.

Once, she'd fancied herself in love with a man working a job near Fool's Gold, only to discover he was a liar and a cheat.

There had been men who'd come onto her in the bar, but she'd had little time to return their advances, working as a bartender at night and guiding trail tours during the day. They'd lost interest. She'd never really had interest in any of them.

But Jake…

Now here was a quiet man with eyes that had seen pain. What kind of pain, RJ couldn't imagine.

As a bartender, she'd listened to so many men and women pour out their hearts, as if she were the therapist like her friend Emily. She'd listened, realizing that, sometimes, that was all the customers needed.

Staring into Jake's dark, haunted eyes, she'd gladly listen to his story. Her curiosity was piqued by the big guy who favored his left leg. What was his story? What had been the source of his injury? Did he have a woman waiting for him somewhere?

That last thought hit her square in the chest. No. She wasn't interested in Jake Cogburn. Just because he'd saved her life didn't mean she should hero-worship him.

"RJ, I know you can handle any of the weapons we have on the ranch," Gunny was saying, bringing her back out of her thoughts about Jake. "But you don't have anyone to keep an eye on you. You're always going. You don't have time to look over your shoulder."

"It's my life," she said. Not with regret or disgust. Just the facts. "I don't have time to slow down, either."

"Then you agree," her father said, a smile teasing the corners of his mouth.

Her eyes narrowed. "Agree to what?"

"That you need a bodyguard."

"What?" She stepped back. "No. I don't agree to any such thing. And we don't have the money to hire one, anyway."

"You don't have to hire one," Kujo said. "Jake is available, and his first assignment as a new member of the Brotherhood Protectors Colorado team, will be to protect you until they can find the guy who murdered Henderson."

"Whoa!" RJ held up both hands. "I don't need a bodyguard. And I'm sure Mr. Cogburn has better things to do than babysit a grown woman who doesn't need a shadow following her around. Besides, I have too much to do. He'd be in the way."

Gunny slapped his palm on the bar. "He's got the job." Her father turned to Jake. "Thank you. I'd follow her around, but I'm not as young as I used to be, and I've got all the chores she isn't doing to get done. This place takes a lot of upkeep."

"We'll work out the details over those steaks."

Kujo glanced around the bar. "Looks like the sheriff and state police are releasing the customers to go home."

Still hot about being forced to accept a bodyguard's protection, RJ spun and went back to work, scrubbing counters, cleaning glassware and sweeping the room with JoJo's assistance.

JoJo brought her more empty cups and mugs and set them on the counter. "Are you up to the Pioneer Days events next weekend," JoJo asked.

RJ frowned, her hand stopping the wiping motion she'd employed on the shiny wooden bar. "Of course. Why shouldn't I be?"

"Well, after nearly being killed tonight, I thought you might want to pass on being Madame LaBelle for the ghost town show."

"Other than wearing a dress, there's nothing keeping me from performing my part. Although how you talked me into it, I'll never know."

"You'll be great. And you're the only woman I know who can convincingly pull off a gunfight in a dress."

"I don't know about that."

"At the very least, no one will recognize you in anything other than jeans." JoJo tilted her head. "When was the last time you wore a dress or a skirt?" JoJo nodded her head toward the jean skirt RJ wore. "By the way, you've got great legs. You should wear dresses more often."

RJ tugged at the skirt. "I don't like wearing girlie

clothes."

JoJo laughed. "Why? Afraid someone might mistake you for being female?"

"I'm more afraid they'll think I can't take care of myself." She shot an angry glance toward the table Kujo and Jake had moved to. "Why can't people leave things the way they are?"

JoJo frowned. "I get the feeling we're not talking about dresses and skirts anymore." She leaned across the counter and touched RJ's arm. "What's wrong?"

"Nothing," RJ bit out. "Not a damned thing."

"Seriously, you look like you're ready to bite someone's head off." JoJo glanced around. "Who's got your panties in a wad? I'll take care of him for you."

RJ's gaze automatically went to Jake.

The man's gaze met hers. Had he been watching her all along? Was he already performing his role as a bodyguard?

"Is it Jake?" JoJo's hands balled into fists. "Let me at him." She abandoned her tray and stalked across the room, plopping into the chair beside the man who'd saved RJ's life and was now going to make it miserable by following her around like a lost puppy.

RJ glanced down at Striker, sitting on the floor beside her. "I already have a lost puppy. I don't need another one following me around, do I?" She ruffled Striker's ears. "You're the only boy I need in my life." Her glance shot to Jake, and warmth spread throughout her body. Why? She hadn't a clue.

Her lips quirked upward as JoJo leaned into the

man, her face fierce, her fists still clenched. "Go get 'em, JoJo," she whispered. What she wouldn't give to be a fly on that table and hear her friend take the man down a notch or two.

Forcing her gaze away from the table where her bodyguard and best friend sat, RJ went back to work. As customers were screened by the police and left, tables emptied. RJ helped Gunny stack chairs upside down on tabletops. Soon, the place was empty but for Gunny, Kujo, Jake, RJ and JoJo.

Deputy Gathright entered through the front door of the bar and crossed to where Gunny stood.

RJ's father propped his broom against the bar and held out his hand. "Deputy, thank you for coming and getting the state police involved."

"We're looking for the perpetrator," Gathright said. "As soon as we hear anything, we'll be in touch. In the meantime, keep an ear open and your eyes peeled. I'd hate to get another call and this time have it be you or your daughter."

"We're taking care of it," Gunny assured the deputy.

"Good. We're out of here. They've loaded the victim into the ambulance and are taking him to the county morgue. The state police have already left. I hope your night gets better." He shook hands with Gunny, tipped his hat toward RJ and JoJo and left.

RJ hurried after him. "Ray," she called out.

The deputy stopped and turned. "Ma'am?"

"Could you follow JoJo home?" RJ asked. "I don't

want anything to happen to her."

"I'll be all right," JoJo said, slinging her purse over her shoulder. "But he can follow me into Fool's Gold."

Ray nodded and held the door for JoJo.

RJ's friend paused in front of her. "For the record, I'm glad Jake's going to be your bodyguard. He's all right. Give him a chance. He could surely use it."

Before RJ could protest, JoJo was out the door, following the deputy to her vehicle.

RJ finished with the mopping and carried the bucket and mop to the back door.

Juggling the two items into one hand, she reached out to open the back door.

Before she could reach for the doorknob, another hand slipped around her and opened the door for her. "Let me go first," a deep, familiar voice said.

Jake eased past her, his shoulders bumping against hers, sending shock waves of awareness through her body.

She stood for a moment, trying and failing at getting a grip on the sensations contact with the man inspired.

As she hesitated, Striker wove between her legs and leaped off the back steps. He sniffed Jake's leg then sat beside the man, looking up at her expectantly.

"Traitor." Could she put up with Jake shadowing her every move? And for how long?

"Oh, hell no," she murmured.

CHAPTER 4

JAKE HEARD her muttered words and fought the first grin he could remember since he'd learned he'd lost his leg.

He liked that she was strong and knew her own mind. But this woman's stubborn independence might get her killed...if he let it happen.

"Sorry," he murmured. "You're not dying on my watch."

"I'm not dying anytime soon." She hung the mop on a hook outside the back door. For a moment, she stood on the top step, her chin held high, her hair falling in soft waves around her shoulders.

A light breeze lifted the curls, giving her the appearance of an avenging angel.

Jake's groin tightened. The woman was tough, yet utterly feminine. However, if he said that out loud, she'd probably take offense.

Her lips pursed. "I'm not going to shake you, am I?"

He crossed his arms over his chest and shook his head. "You heard Gunny. I've been hired to protect you."

"And I'm telling you. I don't need protection."

"You did earlier this evening," he pointed out.

"I wasn't expecting to be attacked."

"You can't be on guard at all times. Even on the SEAL team, we had each other's backs. No man, or woman, has eyes in the back of his or her head."

"You were a Navy SEAL?" RJ descended the porch steps to the ground and looked up into his eyes.

His chest tightened. "Yes, ma'am."

"Why did you leave the Navy?"

"Wasn't my choice," he bit out.

Her eyes narrowed, and she studied him in the light cast by the yellow bulb over the back porch.

She didn't need to know the circumstances of his forced retirement. All she needed to know was that he could do the job.

Finally, she sighed. "I don't like being followed."

"I'm not all that sure I'll like dogging your footsteps. But this is my job, now, and I'm going to do it, whether you like it or not." He cocked an eyebrow, inviting her to disagree.

"Fine." She lifted her chin. "I'm not slowing down for you to keep up."

His jaw hardened. Jake had never been the one to hold up the team. He certainly wouldn't hold up this female. "I don't expect you to slow down for me. I'll keep up."

"Have you ever been on a horse?" she asked.

His eyes narrowed. "A few times, why?"

"I'm leading a trail ride tomorrow. I won't have time to saddle your horse or teach you how to ride. I'll have my hands full with ranch guests."

"You won't have to take care of me. I'll manage on my own." God, he hoped he could.

Since losing his leg, he hadn't been in a saddle. Growing up, he'd had a friend whose family had a small ranch in Cañon City. They'd gone there on weekends to ride and explore the foothills.

That had been a long time ago. Surely, riding a horse was like riding a bicycle. Once you learned how, you just knew.

The big difference was that he now had a prosthetic device in place of a foot and lower leg. He wasn't entirely sure how he'd mount the horse once he got it saddled. He'd have to get out to the barn that night or early the next morning to practice. "What time is the trail ride?"

"Ten o'clock. I have six guests riding with us."

He nodded. "And me. I'm coming with you."

She shrugged. "Suit yourself." She tipped her head toward the lodge. "Has Gunny shown you and your partner to your rooms?"

He shook his head. "No. We were busy looking over the lodge facilities and the barn when I came back to the barn for a couple of beers."

"Remind me to stock the lodge refrigerator," she said. "I usually have some beer there for the guests."

"It's a good thing there weren't any today." He couldn't imagine what would've happened if he hadn't wanted that beer, and if there had been some in the refrigerator. Having lost one person to the attacker was bad enough. If RJ had died because of her attacker...

Jake had wallowed far too long in his own self-pity. He'd lost his leg. Not his life. It was time he pulled himself up by his bootstraps and got on with the business of living.

So, he wasn't with his Navy SEAL team anymore. He was needed here on the Lost Valley Ranch. RJ might not think so, but she needed someone to have her back, to be there in case the killer returned to make sure she didn't remember his face.

The back door to the bar opened. "All done inside and locked up," Gunny announced. "Didn't like closing up early, but now, we can get to those steaks."

Kujo stepped around Gunny and joined Jake and RJ on the ground below the steps.

Gunny locked the back door, and the four of them walked across the grass to the lodge.

Inside, several guests were in the great room enjoying a card game. They asked about the emergency vehicles and were shocked at what Gunny told them.

"Anyone need some coffee, tea or hot cocoa?" RJ asked, hoping to calm the guests.

The group answered with their choices, and RJ hurried to the kitchen to accommodate them. Her dog followed as if he was used to helping. The animal walked with a limp. Upon closer inspection, Jake notice Striker was missing a foot.

They had something in common. The thought gave Jake something to think about.

Jake trailed behind the pair, pushing through the swinging door to find RJ at the refrigerator and her dog lying on a cushion beside a small kitchen table.

"If you're going to follow me around, make yourself useful." RJ pointed to the coffee pot. "You can start a pot of fresh coffee while I get those steaks out of the refrigerator and prepped for the oven."

"Aye, aye!" With her directions to the filters and coffee grounds, he managed to load the coffeemaker and get the water percolating.

"Some of them wanted hot cocoa," he noted. "Point, and I'll prepare."

RJ straightened from grabbing four large potatoes out of a bin near the sink and motioned with her elbow to the cabinet above the coffeemaker. "The cocoa is in the cabinet in front of you. Mugs are in the one next to it. There's a tray on the counter behind you."

RJ poked holes in the potatoes and placed them in the microwave. "Don't judge me."

"For putting potatoes in the microwave?" He shook his head. "Takes too long in the oven when you're in a hurry."

"You cook much?"

He lifted a shoulder. "Enough to know how to bake a potato in the microwave."

While he filled cups with hot water from the teapot on the stove and mixed in the cocoa powder, RJ cut up lettuce, tomatoes and onions into a salad and laid out plates.

When the coffee was finished brewing, Jake poured it into the waiting mugs and set the coffee and the hot cocoa on the tray, added a small pitcher of cream, spoons and a bowl of sugar. "If you'll open the door, I'll carry this out."

RJ rinsed her hands in the sink, dried them and pushed through the swinging kitchen door, holding it open with her hip as Jake walked through.

The group at the card table gave a happy cheer.

RJ helped Jake serve the drinks and returned with him to the kitchen.

Gunny was there, placing the steaks on a broiler. "I've got this if you want to set the table. And you might want to show Jake and Kujo where they'll be staying tonight."

RJ nodded. "Check the potatoes in the microwave. I'll be back in a minute." She grabbed plates and silverware and slowed as she passed Jake. "Grab the salad and follow me."

The woman knew how to give orders.

Jake didn't have a problem following them. He scooped up the bowl with the salad and the bottles of dressing she'd set beside it and followed her and her ever-present dog through to the dining room.

Within seconds, she had the plates and silverware laid out.

"We have a few minutes before the steaks will be done. I can show you where you and your partner can sleep."

Jake followed her back through the great room to the staircase.

Kujo entered the front door, carrying Jake's duffel bag and one of his own.

"Good timing," RJ said. "If you'll come with me, I'll show you to your rooms." Without waiting, she climbed the stairs, her Malinois beside her.

Jake took his bag from Kujo and slung it over his shoulder.

Kujo followed RJ up the stairs, and Jake brought up the rear, doing his best not to give any indication that he was different. It wasn't easy, but he climbed the stairs almost as smoothly as Kujo and RJ. The prosthesis rubbing against his stump had begun to hurt, but he didn't let it show.

Ahead of him, RJ turned a knob and pushed open a door. "This room has an adjoining bathroom. You'll find fresh towels in a basket by the shower."

Kujo entered and set his bag on a chair in the corner.

RJ continued down the hall and opened the next door. "Sorry, but this room shares the bathroom across the hall."

Jake entered the room and dropped his bag on the floor. When he turned, he found RJ watching him, her gaze on his leg.

He stiffened and waited for her to say something about his limp. When she didn't, he let go of the breath he hadn't realized he'd been holding.

RJ nodded toward the dresser. "There are towels in the top drawer. If you need any shaving cream or a spare toothbrush, there's some in a basket in the bathroom. You can help yourself."

"Thank you. I brought my own."

"The steaks should be ready soon. Don't be long."

"I'll go down with Miss Tate. If you'd like to wash up," Kujo said from the hallway.

Jake nodded. "Thanks. I'll be down shortly."

When RJ and Kujo left, Jake carried his bag to the bathroom across the hall. He found his electric clippers, toothbrush and a set of relatively clean clothes. Stripping out of the Led Zeppelin T-shirt, he sat on the side of the bathtub and slipped out of his prosthetic, and then his jeans.

When he pushed to his foot, he glanced at the mirror, shocked at the scruffy man staring back at him. Damn he needed a haircut, shower and shave. The haircut would have to wait. If he hurried, he could take care of the rest before he returned to the dining room.

Jake set his clippers on four and ran it across his heavy beard, taking it down to a little more than a shadow. As a SEAL, he'd always worn a beard, unless the mission called for a clean shave. Within minutes, he had his beard trimmed and neat. He couldn't do much about his hair until he made it to a barber.

Once he cleaned off the counter, he eased his leg over the edge of the top of the tub and stood in the shower, letting the hot water wash away the stench of poor living. Using a fresh bar of soap, he scrubbed himself from head to toe, rinsed and scrubbed again.

By the time he left the shower, he felt—and smelled—like a new man.

Less than five minutes later, he'd brushed his teeth, dressed and was on his way down the stairs, taking one step at a time. Going down was always trickier than climbing up. He held on tightly to the handrail and made it to the bottom without plunging to his death. As challenging as it had been, he couldn't let RJ see that he struggled with anything as simple as descending a staircase.

She was the strong one in this situation. How could he help keep her safe?

An image of a man straddling her, holding his hand over her mouth and nose, suffocating the life out of her, reminded Jake that he had stopped the man from killing her. He'd pulled him off and flung him aside. Jake had breathed air back into her lungs and kept her from dying.

He had purpose. His life hadn't ended when he'd lost his leg. Not a very superstitious sort, he was beginning to believe everything that had happened to him had been for a bigger reason than simply getting him kicked out of the Navy. Could it be he was supposed to be at the Lost Valley Ranch, and that he was meant to go for that beer he hadn't really needed?

Jake shook his head. For whatever reason he was there, he had a job to perform. And that job was to protect the woman who'd witnessed a murder.

RJ HELPED her father fill glasses with ice, load the juicy medium rare steaks onto a platter and carry them into the dining room.

Kujo carried in the pitcher of iced tea and a pot of coffee. When dinner was ready, RJ frowned. "Do you think Jake got lost?"

Kujo laughed. "This lodge is not that big. I'm sure he'll be here momentarily."

Jake chose that moment to appear in the doorway to the dining room. His longish dark hair was slicked back and damp, and he wore a white polo shirt with his jeans and boots. The scraggly beard was gone. In its place was a neatly trimmed beard.

RJ's heart fluttered. The man was ruggedly handsome enough he could have any woman he desired.

And he'd given her the kiss of life.

She shook her head slightly. No. He'd given her mouth-to-mouth. It didn't count as a kiss. Especially since she'd almost been unconscious when he'd administered the technique.

RJ found herself wondering what it would feel

like to have his lips on hers for a real kiss. Her lips tingled at the thought. Something deep in her core coiled into a tight knot.

Dragging her gaze away from the man, she announced, "Dinner's ready. Please take a seat."

RJ stood behind the chair to the right of where her father sat at the head of the table. Kujo sat to the left of RJ's father.

Jake held RJ's chair and waited as she sat and scooted forward. Then he claimed the chair beside her.

Unused to having someone else attend to her chair, RJ felt heat rising in her cheeks. "Holding my chair isn't necessary. You're the guest here."

"My mother would beg to differ," Jake said, and then murmured beneath his breath, "may she rest in peace."

"I'm sorry for your loss," RJ said. "And thank you. Your mother would've been proud."

"I don't know about that." Jake dropped onto the chair beside her and reached for the platter of baked potatoes, offering her one before he took one for himself.

"How long has she been gone?" RJ asked as she cut her potato down the middle and loaded it with pats of butter, salt and pepper.

"She passed eight years ago, while I was deployed to Iraq."

"I'm sorry. That must've been hard."

Jake nodded without saying anything.

"Would you like sour cream for your potato?" RJ asked, reaching for the tub of sour cream.

"No thank you," Jake said. "I like it with just butter, salt and pepper."

RJ smiled. "Me, too."

"RJ," Kujo said. "Your father tells me you two run this ranch by yourselves."

"We do," she answered, stabbing her fork into one of the steaks on the platter. "Except for the bar staff, it's just the two of us. I take it you've decided to rent the lodge."

Kujo nodded. "I think it'll work for what Hank has in mind. With a few modifications, the basement is large enough for our operations. Jake will be running the show after I leave, if he chooses to accept the responsibility."

"Exactly what kind of operation are you going to operate?" RJ sliced her knife through the steak and cut off a small bite.

Kujo took one of the steaks from the platter and placed it on his plate. "We're a security firm. We provide protection and other resources to people in need who can't get enough assistance from the authorities."

"So, is Jake on a test run?" RJ asked, her gaze going to the man beside her. "Or are you testing the organization before you decide if it's worth taking charge?"

"A little of both," Jake said quietly.

"What about the rest of the Lost Valley Ranch

operations?" RJ's glance went back to Kujo. "If we shut down for a year to accommodate your lease, we risk losing our return customers. We start all over from scratch building our clientele."

Kujo nodded. "We want you to keep running your operations, less the space we're renting. That way if, at the end of our year, we decide an office in Colorado isn't viable, you won't lose customers and can carry on business as usual without the Brotherhood Protectors taking up your space."

"Fair enough," RJ said.

"Your ranching operations will provide cover for our guys. Not that we're all that covert, but it does help. And as the men and women we hire wait for their assignments, they'll assist with the ranch and bar duties."

"We can't pay them for assisting," RJ was quick to point out.

"You won't have to. Hank Patterson will pay the team and the rental amount. Our guys will work for free on the ranch. You just can't rely too much on them as they'll be assigned out to whatever project comes along."

RJ frowned. "This deal sounds too good to be true. A big lease payment and free help? What's the catch?"

Kujo laughed. "No catch. We just want a place to base our branch of the Brotherhood Protectors. Hank trusts Gunny...and if you're anything like your father, we can trust you."

Gunny snorted. "She's just as hard-headed, if that counts. And as mouthy."

Heat filled RJ's cheeks as she glared at her father. "Thanks for the vote of confidence."

His face straightened. "Seriously, you won't find anyone as trustworthy and caring as my Rucker. The one thing she doesn't get from me is her looks." His expression softened. "She's beautiful, like her mother."

"She is," Jake agreed, his voice so quiet RJ almost missed his words.

The heat intensified in her cheeks. "My looks have nothing to do with this conversation. What's the next step in this agreement?"

"Hank sent a written contract with me," Kujo said. "You can take it, review it and let me know what changes you'd like to make. I'm authorized to write a check for the first and last month's rent and to start the contracting services we'll need to set up the computer network and security system we require." He started to get up from the table.

Gunny's hand shot out and caught Kujo's arm. "No need to do the paperwork now. That steak isn't getting any warmer. Eat before it's cold."

"Yes, sir," Kujo said and sliced off a piece of the tender meat and stuck it in his mouth.

RJ stopped eating halfway through her steak. Sitting so close to Jake made her uncomfortable. He wasn't any closer than her father or Kujo, but he was a big guy. The breadth of his shoulders alone left little space between him and RJ.

Every time she moved her arm, it brushed against his, sending a shock of awareness through her body.

She cleared her throat. "If you'll excuse me, I'm going to bed. I have a busy day tomorrow, and it starts early."

"What time?" Jake asked.

"I'm up by five-thirty to get the animals fed before we start breakfast for our guests."

"And the trail ride is at ten?" Jake affirmed.

"Yes." RJ pushed back from the table. "Gentlemen. We look forward to doing business with the Brotherhood Protectors. Thank you for considering Lost Valley Ranch. Anything you need, let me know. In the meantime, I'm calling it a night."

Her father stood. "I'll take care of kitchen cleanup. Leave your plate." He walked with her to the base of the staircase where he opened his arms. "It's been a rough day."

She went into those strong arms and wrapped her arms around her father's waist. It wasn't often he showed affection. He didn't have to. RJ knew how much he loved her. Giving up his career as a fighting Marine to take on a recruiting position so that she could stay in one place throughout high school had been evidence enough. Still, those hugs were few and far between. She'd take it. Even with an audience.

"I'm glad you're okay," Gunny whispered.

"Me too," she whispered back.

He leaned away and brushed a strand of her hair from her face "You remind me so much of your mother. Juliet would've been so proud of you."

"I wish I could've known her."

"You would've loved her. She would've done a much better job of raising you."

"Don't knock yourself. As far as I'm concerned, you've done a great job." She kissed her father's cheek. "Love ya, Dad."

He kissed her forehead. "Love you, too, Jules."

He didn't call her Jules often, and it was when he was thinking of her mother. RJ having almost lost her life had to have hit him hard. She smiled. "Don't worry, Dad. I'm not going anywhere."

"If you do, let it be on your own terms. I want you to get away from here, see the world and experience all that life has to offer. You've been too tied down with the ranch and the bar."

"I wouldn't be here if I didn't love it."

"Yeah, but sometimes, I think we hold you back." He stepped away. "Maybe having the steady income from the Brotherhood Protectors will allow me to hire some help. You can go wherever you desire."

Her lips twisted. "Trying to get rid of me?"

"No. Of course not." He sighed. "I remember how excited you were to join the Army. You were going to see the world."

"And then, I didn't." She nodded. "I have no regrets. I love this ranch and the people who come to stay. Most of all, I love you."

"Just promise me..." her father said. "You won't pass up an opportunity to see the world, to get out of here and be open to a different life, if that's what you want."

"Dad..." RJ started.

"Promise me. Your mother had so many plans to see the world with me. She never got that chance."

RJ's chest squeezed hard. "Because of me."

Her father's brow dipped low. "Don't."

"If she hadn't had me, she would still be alive today."

"Your mother wanted you more than anything in the world. She loved you from the day she learned she was pregnant. To her, there was no choice. She wanted you to be born and live a full and happy life. Don't ever blame yourself for her death." He gripped her arms. "Do you hear me? Don't ever."

Tears welled in RJ's eyes. She blinked them back. Her tough Marine father didn't tolerate tears. "Okay. And I promise, if an occasion arises that I want to leave and travel the world, I won't hesitate. But I'll always come back. Because my heart is here with you." She hugged him.

"Your heart won't always be only with me."

She smiled at her father. "There isn't a man in this world who can live up to the bar you've set."

"Don't be so sure." His gaze went to the table they'd left behind.

In the corner of her eye, she caught movement through the door of the dining room.

Jake stood with his plate, stacking her plate on it and her father's after that. He carried it into the kitchen, limping slightly.

She was thankful Jake had come along when he had. The man had saved her life. But anything more than that? RJ gave her father a narrow-eyed glare. "Don't go playing matchmaker. Those men are here on business. I'm just a job to them. Besides, I'm not in the market for a relationship. I have enough to do without one."

Her father shook his head. "I'm not playing matchmaker. But you should keep your options open on that account as well. Kujo and Jake are what heroes are made of. They're the real deal."

"Dad, you're all the hero I need."

"Hell, Jules, Jake saved your life. Not many men would step into the fray like that. And not many would know how to revive a person who's been suffocated."

"I owe him my life, but that doesn't mean I have to fall in love with him. And Kujo's married and has a baby on the way." She patted her father's arm. "Nice try, though. I'm going to get a shower and go to bed. I have a full day tomorrow."

"Get some sleep, Jules." He hugged her again and set her at arm's length, his hands holding her arms. "And while you're at it, think about what I've said."

"Okay. Okay." She smiled. "You're a pushy bastard, aren't you?"

"Only when it counts."

"Only when you want it your way."

"When it comes to the happiness of my only child, you're damn right." He winked. "Go. Get that shower and the sleep you need after the day you've had."

"Love you, Dad."

"Love you, too."

RJ hurried up the stairs. With so many things going through her mind, she doubted seriously she'd be able to go to sleep anytime soon.

A shiver slithered down her spine at the remembered feeling of being overpowered and helpless when she'd been attacked. She could have died tonight.

And then she remembered the feeling of having life breathed back into her and the face of the man who'd saved her. Was it possible to mistake hero worship for love? Not that she was in love with a perfect stranger. Hell, she'd never been in love. She wouldn't know what it felt like if it bit her in the ass.

RJ turned the shower on full blast and as hot as she could stand it, hoping to relax beneath the spray. All she managed to do was make her skin wrinkled and pink. She was no closer to sleep than she had been before the shower. Instead of sleepy, RJ was itchy, on the edge and...aroused.

CHAPTER 5

Jake and Kujo helped Gunny clean the kitchen and put away dishes and pans.

"Thank you," Gunny said. "I'm used to RJ and me being the only ones pulling kitchen duty."

"We don't want to add to your workload," Kujo said. "We're just happy to have a place to work out of that makes sense for our operation."

"I'm realistic. It solves a lot of our issues, having a steady income with the rent Hank's willing to pay." Gunny hung a dish towel on the oven rail and nodded. "Thanks for the help. Anything you need, help yourself."

"I'd like to make the rounds of the exterior of the lodge and the barn before I call it a night," Jake said. He glanced at Kujo.

"I'll keep an eye on RJ while you're out there. Take your time."

Jake nodded. "Thanks. I might be a while. I want

to familiarize with the layout at night as well as during the day."

"We have RJ covered, and you have a key card to let yourself in the front door," Gunny said. "Have a good night. This geezer needs his beauty sleep. Oh, and be aware. You're in the Colorado mountains. Be on the lookout for bear."

Jake let himself out the front door. Motion-sensor lights blinked on as he walked around the outside of the lodge. The barn stood a little away from the building. As he walked down to the barn, another motion-sensor light blinked on.

Gunny had done well with the lighting. Not only would the lights be good for guests to get around, but they would also come on if animals were moving around at night. Bears were a real threat. Even in the nearby city of Colorado Springs, they'd had reports of bears in housing developments.

One woman had had an inflatable children's pool set up in her fenced backyard. When she'd come home for lunch one day, she'd surprised a bear playing in the pool. Jake could imagine the woman's reaction. The bear, like its human counterpart, had only been looking for a place to cool off.

Jake entered the barn, switched on the interior lights and closed the door behind him.

The barn had ten stalls, five on each side. Each stall was filled with a horse. They greeted him with soft nickers. A couple pawed the ground.

"Which one of you wants to let me practice on you?" he asked.

More nickers.

He studied each of the horses, passing in front of their stalls.

A bay gelding put his head over the door of his stall and reached out, snuffling. Probably looking for a carrot or apple.

Jake made a note to bring a treat from the kitchen the next time he came to the barn.

The gelding appeared big enough to carry him and calm enough to put up with Jake's clumsy attempts to ride with a prosthesis. He hoped he was right.

Jake took a lead rope from a hook on the wall and clipped it onto the gelding's halter. He opened the stall door and led the animal out into the center of the barn where he found a place to tie him.

A door near the front of the barn led into the tack room where saddles were arranged on saddle trees, neat and well-maintained. The leather on each was worn, but in good condition.

Passing the saddles, he grabbed a brush and a curry comb and returned to the horse.

Jake took his time brushing the animal's coat, letting the animal get used to him. When he was satisfied with the time and effort, he returned the brush and curry comb to the tack room.

He selected a saddle blanket from a stack in a

corner, a bridle and saddle that was large enough for a man his size and carried his finds out to the horse.

"I wish I knew your name," he said as he spread the blanket on the animal's back. It had been at least ten years since he'd saddled a horse, but the motions easily came back to him.

After the blanket, he slung the saddle over the animal's back and reached beneath his belly to fit the leather strap through the metal ring on the girth and pulled tight. Looping the strap back through the saddle and again through the girth, he tugged until the girth was good and tight. He didn't want to place his foot in the stirrup and have the saddle slide around the horse, dumping him on the ground.

With the horse still tied securely to a post, Jake placed his prosthetic foot in the stirrup, reached up, grabbed the saddle horn and pulled himself up into the seat. So far, so good.

Sitting in the saddle felt as natural as it had when he'd been a teenager riding through the hills with his friend. In the saddle, he didn't limp. He was on almost equal footing with any other rider. It felt good. Empowering.

Hope dared to swell in his chest.

How long had it been since he'd felt anything other than despair?

Jake sat for a long time, overwhelmed by what he was feeling and glad he'd come out to the barn by himself to practice before he set out on a trail ride the following day. He was absolutely determined not to slow down RJ in any way. If he wanted to be effective as a bodyguard, he had to be right there with her at all times.

Dismounting turned out to be less of a success than mounting. A noise near the door made the horse sidestep in the middle of the dismount.

Jake's boot on his prosthetic leg slipped too deep into the stirrup and kept him from pulling it free.

The horse danced sideways and nickered.

Thankfully, Jake still had hold of the saddle horn. He hopped on his good foot until he could get the horse to settle and he could pull his prosthetic boot free of the stirrup. The device had turned cock-eyed and required him to hike his pant leg up to readjust it and get it on straight again.

Once he was back on track, Jake slipped the bridle between the gelding's teeth and up over his ears, adjusting it to fit. This time, when he mounted, the horse wouldn't be tied to a post. Jake had to be able to mount in the open.

He practiced several times, still having to place his foot in the stirrup, careful not to let the boot slip too far in. After several times up and down, he felt better about his ability to manage on his own.

Jake removed the saddle, bridle and blanket. Brushed the gelding and led him back into his stall. He found a bucket of feed and gave him a little extra for putting up with his practice session.

He'd be ready for the trail ride the following day. He couldn't be worrying about mounting or keeping his seat in the saddle. Not when he had to keep an eye out for someone who might attack RJ. The pretty rancher had escaped death once. Jake would be damned if someone got past him to finish what he'd started.

RJ EASED AWAY from the barn door and retraced her footsteps back to the lodge, Striker trotting alongside her, keeping pace.

He made a low rumbling sound deep in his chest as a warning.

He hadn't needed to. RJ knew who was out there. She'd seen him leave the lodge shortly after she had.

"I know you're following me," she said as she climbed the steps to the wide back porch. "You don't have to hide."

Kujo emerged from the shadows and followed her up the steps. "Did you see enough?" he asked.

RJ paced the length of the porch and back. "Why didn't he say something?"

"And what would you have him say?" Kujo leaned against a post and crossed his arms over his chest. "I'm missing a leg? I was kicked out of the Navy SEALs because I can't meet the physical standards that include two functioning arms and two functioning legs? That my whole life has changed, and I don't fit in with the civilian world?"

"No, of course not." RJ stopped in front of Kujo.

"But he could've let me know. He doesn't have to come on the trail ride tomorrow."

"Are you kidding? The last thing Jake needs is your pity. That man is out there practicing his mount and dismount so that he can perform his job without showing weakness. Don't take that away from him. He can do anything a man with two legs can. He just has to figure that out for himself."

RJ's chest tightened. She could only imagine the shock and devastation of losing a limb and how hard it must be for Jake to find a new normal.

Kujo straightened. "Here he comes. Are you going to say anything to him?"

RJ wanted to ask Jake about his injury. To do so, she'd have to admit she'd spied on him in the barn. And what did one say to someone who'd lost so much?

Sorry you lost your leg seemed so banal and useless.

Kujo was right.

"I'm not going to say anything," RJ whispered. She studied Jake as he crossed the yard, limping slightly. She would never have suspected he had a fake leg. He hid it well.

As he approached the porch, he frowned up at her. "I thought you were going to bed?"

RJ shrugged. "I couldn't sleep."

Jake nodded to Kujo. "I'll take over from here."

"Thanks," Kujo said. "I need to phone home and see how Molly's doing without me. She said the baby's been really active at night, keeping her awake."

"Go," RJ said. "I don't plan on being out here much longer."

Kujo lifted his chin toward Jake. "Goodnight, then." He entered the lodge, closing the door behind him.

RJ stared at Jake for a long moment, wishing the man would open up to her and tell her about what had happened. That way everything would be out in the open, and she wouldn't have to walk on eggshells, avoiding the obvious.

"Still thinking about the attack?" Jake asked.

"That and everything else that has happened today."

"You know we'll do the best we can to keep that man from getting to you again," Jake said.

RJ nodded. "I believe that." And she did. She'd read articles and watched shows about Navy SEALs. Those men were badass tough. Not only did they go through hell in training, they also deployed often and into some of the most dangerous and hostile environments imaginable.

Many lost their lives in the line of duty. Despite losing his leg, Jake was one of the lucky ones to return home, and not in a body bag.

RJ wanted to tell him that. Knowing he'd lost a leg explained the shadows in his eyes and the fact he didn't smile much.

Kujo said he was still trying to figure out how he fit into the civilian world. The man had probably been in the Navy since he'd graduated high school.

Most likely he didn't know any other life but the military. And he would be missing his teammates.

RJ's hand went automatically to Striker's soft head. She relied on the animal for more than protection. He was her friend when she didn't have time for the human kind. The dog was her constant companion since she'd adopted him. Jake could use a companion like Striker. The dog laid on the porch and rested his chin on his paws. Sometimes, RJ wished she had Striker's life. Work when you needed to and nap every chance you got.

Striker still had issues from his time serving in the military. He was missing his back paw and loud noises frightened him. He'd come a long way from the dog she'd picked up at the kennel at the Air Force Academy in Colorado Springs.

RJ's friend Emily worked with men and women who suffered with Post Traumatic Stress Disorder. They'd been exposed to trauma most civilians would never encounter. She worked with people who had trouble assimilating into a life without the military. Many didn't make the transition and opted for suicide.

RJ's gut knotted. Jake had every reason to want to end his life. That he hadn't didn't mean he hadn't thought about it. And he'd gone the extra mile to practice getting up in the saddle and back down, just to prove to himself he could do it without falling flat on his ass. He wasn't ready to quit.

Her estimation of Jake Cogburn jumped up

several notches. The man was trying, which was a lot more than some folks who hadn't been hit with everything he had.

"You're very lucky," Jake said.

His words pulled RJ out of her internal musings and back to the man in front of her. "How so?"

"This place is amazing. Everywhere you look, you see mountains and nature."

"And work." She sighed. "Lots of work."

"Like Kujo said, the Brotherhood Protectors will help when we can."

"So, does that mean you're going to take the job?" RJ realized that if he did, she'd be seeing a lot more of him. Her pulse fluttered.

He stared out into the darkness. "I haven't made up my mind."

"Sounds like Kujo needs to get back to his wife. I can't imagine her letting him go so far away when she's pregnant."

"From what Kujo's told me, she's pretty tough," Jake said. "She's a special agent with the FBI."

"Well then, she can handle things on her own." RJ shook her head. "I do a lot of things around here, but I still think that, if I were pregnant, I might want my spouse to be close by."

"Kujo won't say it, but I think he'd rather be back in Montana with Molly. But he has great respect for Hank Patterson and the Brotherhood Protectors." Jake shook his head. "I don't know why they think

I'm the man to lead the Colorado Office, but here I am." He raised his hands, palms up.

"Sounds like you're fairly impressed with what they do."

His lips twitched at the corners. "I'll let you know after your current dilemma is resolved and you're still standing. In the meantime, the stars seem to be brighter here than anywhere else in the world."

"Probably because you're closer to them, and there isn't a lot of light pollution out here." RJ leaned against the porch rail and stared up at the night sky. "I love this ranch and Colorado. My father thinks I need to leave here and explore the world." She turned to him. "What do you think?"

"I think you need to be where you're happy. Only you can decide where that is."

"Agreed. I'm a firm believer that you are the only person who can make yourself happy. Places are just a part of the equation. Anyone can be happy, if she sets her mind to it, no matter where she is."

Jake chuckled. "Look at us being all philosophical."

"Maybe that's what a brush with death brings out in us."

His brow furrowed.

RJ realized her mistake as soon as the words left her mouth. To retract them would only draw more attention to them and make Jake question what she knew. RJ purposely stared out at the night sky as if nothing was amiss with what she'd said. He didn't know she knew about his leg. When he was ready, he might let her in on his secret. In the meantime, RJ enjoyed standing out in the cool night air with the quiet man.

"How do you feel?" Jake asked into the night.

"Okay," she responded.

"No lingering effects from the attack?"

RJ redirected her gaze to the man who stood beside her, staring into her face in the light from the front porch. Her pulse quickened. "No. Not really—other than my backside is a bit bruised from landing hard on the ground. But I'll live."

Jake touched her chin with his finger, angling her face toward the light. "You might have some bruising where he held his hand over your face."

"I've had worse," she said, her voice breathy. The closer he stood, the less air she seemed able to draw into her lungs. "You should have seen my face after Topper kicked me while cleaning his hooves." She gave a shaky laugh. "I had a huge shiner for weeks." RJ raised a hand to the location of the shiner that was now long gone.

"Horses can be dangerous," Jake said and brushed his thumb across her cheekbone.

"Fighting a war can be a lot more dangerous," she said. "Were you afraid?" Her hand came up to cover his, pressing his warm palm against her skin.

"We didn't have time to be afraid," he said, his voice quiet, his breath fanning across her lips.

His callused hand felt so good, making her sway closer, her body craving the touch of his.

Never had she felt such an intense longing. And this man was a stranger. She glanced up into his face, her brow wrinkling. "Why do you make me feel the way I do?"

He stared down at her, his gaze going to her lips. "What way is that?"

"Confused."

His thumb brushed over her cheek again and then lowered with her hand on his to sweep across her mouth. "Confused?" he whispered.

"And…and…needy." She shook her head slightly.

"What is it you need?" Jake asked, his head lowering until his lips hovered over hers. "This?"

He brushed his mouth across hers, sending a shock of electricity throughout her body and heat coiling at her core.

"Yes," she breathed against him. "But I barely know you."

"Same," he said. "Yet here we are." He leaned his forehead against hers. "And this isn't where we should be." Jake straightened, drew in a deep breath and stepped back. "This shouldn't be happening."

"What shouldn't be happening?" When he'd moved back, the heat his body had produced went with him. Even so, RJ's internal heat burned fiery hot.

"This." He waved a hand between them, shaking

his head. "Please. Accept my apologies. I crossed a line that I shouldn't have."

With her body ignited and her head spinning from his kiss, RJ blinked up at him. "What line?" She looked around them. "What line?"

"I'm working for you as your bodyguard. I can't get so involved with my charge that I lose sight of why I'm here." He took another step backward. "Go to bed, RJ. Forget tonight. It shouldn't have been." He strode to the door, opened it with his key card and held it for her. "Please, go."

RJ schooled her face to poker straight, squared her shoulders and marched toward the door. As she passed him at the threshold, she paused and looked up into his eyes. "You can't undo what happened here. Nor can you wipe it from your memories."

"You're right," he said. "But I can make sure it doesn't happen again."

Anger flared inside. RJ lifted her chin. "Maybe I'll be the one to make sure it doesn't happen. You're just a bodyguard. I'm just the body to be guarded. *The job.* Soon enough, you'll move on. And so will I." RJ passed through the door and sailed up the stairs and into her bedroom, closing the door softly behind her when she really wanted to slam it.

She'd be damned if she showed Jake any kind of emotion. He didn't mean anything to her.

RJ climbed into her bed, pulled the covers up to her chin and steamed. After a few minutes, she shoved the blankets aside and lay there, letting the mountain air cool her heated skin.

The man might just be a bodyguard to her, but damn. He'd made her come alive in the few short hours she'd known him. How the hell was she going to ignore what her body couldn't? And it was highly likely he'd be at Lost Valley Ranch, underfoot, for an entire year.

At that moment, RJ wished her mother were still alive. What she was feeling wasn't something she could talk to Gunny about. And discussing it with JoJo would only make her friend want to push her and the Navy SEAL closer.

Sweet Jesus, help me.

CHAPTER 6

AFTER RJ WENT UP to bed, Jake stepped back out onto the porch, willing his pulse to slow and the tension to ease.

What had he been thinking, kissing the woman? He had no right to come on to her. She was the job. Not to mention, she deserved someone better. Someone who could keep up with her on the ranch.

Jake still wasn't convinced he could hack the rancher life on one leg. Just because he could mount and dismount a horse in a barn didn't mean he could do the same out in the open when the horse would be distracted and likely to dance around with Jake's prosthetic foot caught in the stirrup. Wouldn't that be great?

No.

For a long while, he paced the porch, half-wishing Hank hadn't found him and that Kujo hadn't come to drag him back into the real world.

On the other hand, he felt more alive and useful than he had since he'd woken up in the hospital and was told he'd lost his leg.

And that all had to do with the woman foremost in his mind.

RJ.

The woman had all the experience of a seasoned rancher. But Jake would bet she had little experience with men. Which was all the more reason to keep his hands and lips to himself. She didn't need him hitting on her and...what was it she'd said?

Oh, yeah.

Confusing her.

Hell, she confused *him.*

An hour later, he reentered the lodge, locked the door and climbed the stairs to his room beside the one RJ had gone into. He lay for a long time on his bed, his prothesis within easy reach, his handgun on the nightstand, listening for any sound of distress on the other side of the wall.

Eventually, exhaustion claimed him, and he slept. Several times during the remainder of the night, he woke suddenly, thinking he'd heard something. After listening to the sounds of the old lodge settling, he was reassured and went back to sleep. By five in the morning, he was awake, strapped into his leg and dressed for a day of protecting RJ.

He descended the stairs and followed the light to the kitchen, where a pot of coffee brewed, filling the kitchen with an inviting aroma.

RJ stood with two baking pans in her hands, trying to use her foot to open the oven door. "Would you open the oven for me?"

He hurried forward and pulled open the door of the oven. "Biscuits?"

She nodded and placed the pans on the shelves. "Homemade." After closing the oven, she set the timer and stood back.

Gunny entered the kitchen and sucked in a loud breath. "Nothing smells better than fresh coffee." He nodded to Jake. "Good morning." To RJ, he got right down to business. "What's in the oven?"

"Biscuits. Timer's set. I'm headed out to feed the animals."

"That would be both of us," Jake added. If he hadn't come down when he had, he was certain RJ would've been on her way out alone. "How did you get past me? I was listening."

She met his gaze with a crooked smile. "I like the guests to sleep in so that I can get things done before they come down. I've learned to be stealthy in my movements."

"What time do you rise every morning?"

She shrugged. "When I wake."

"Not helpful," he grumbled. "Can you give me an estimate? If I'm going to provide any protection for you, I have to be with you nearly twenty-four-seven."

"I told you, I don't need a bodyguard." Her chin lifted with that stubborn look she was so good at giving.

"And I told you, too bad," her father said, his jaw firm. "Jake's your shadow, whether you like it or not." Gunny faced Jake. "She rises between four-forty-five and five o'clock every morning. She's done it so long, she doesn't need an alarm."

Jake let slip the smile forming on his lips at the cranky glare RJ shot toward her father.

"Get over it, Jules. I want you alive more than I care if you get mad at me." Her father waved his hands, shooing them toward the door to the dining room. "Go. I can manage breakfast for us and the guests."

RJ left through the back door of the kitchen without waiting for Jake. She was down the porch steps and half-way across the yard before he caught up with her.

"What's first?" Jake asked.

"Feed the horses hay and grain. Fill the water troughs inside the barn and out in the pastures."

Once they had given each horse a couple sections of hay and a bucket of sweet feed, Jake and RJ topped off their water in the barn and in the paddock. All the while, they worked in companionable silence

"Come on," RJ said. "Gunny likes his breakfast hot. He won't start until we're all seated at the table. I don't like cold eggs any more than he does." RJ hurried back to the lodge to help get breakfast out to the guests before they set a platter of scrambled eggs, another of sausage and bacon and another filled with the fluffy biscuits on one of the empty tables in the dining room.

Kujo helped fill glasses with orange juice.

Jake took over filling mugs with coffee or hot water for tea for the guests.

Once everyone was taken care of, they all sat at the table they'd set for the four of them.

"As far as I'm concerned," Gunny said, starting the conversation, "I welcome the Brotherhood Protectors to Lost Valley Ranch." He turned to RJ. "You okay with it?"

RJ's gaze shot to Jake.

For a moment, he thought she would tell Gunny, *no way in hell.*

She lowered her gaze to her plate and nodded. "I'm good with it."

Jake wondered what she meant by that. Was she just acquiescing because her father wanted it? Or was she good with Jake being there for a year and potentially kissing her again?

Assuming he took the job Hank offered.

Did Hank really know how far he'd sunk from his days in the Navy? And if he'd seen him before Kujo had shown up, would he have still offered him a position with the Brotherhood Protectors, much less the lead over the Colorado office?

In a twenty-four-hour timeframe his life had been turned upside down. Did he want to go back to his apartment and drown himself in another beer, and another?

Hell no.

He looked across the table at RJ. If he left, who would take over guarding this woman's welfare? Did he trust anyone else to keep her safe?

And why did he care so much? He didn't really know the woman, other than what he'd observed from the moment he'd breathed life back into her motionless body to the point where he'd kissed her in the starlight.

She was loyal and true to her only family and cared deeply about the ranch they both worked so tirelessly to maintain.

RJ was an extraordinary woman who didn't even recognize how her strength made her incredibly sexy. Some men would find that strength intimidating.

Not Jake.

And he couldn't imagine letting anyone else protect her. At the very least, he'd stick with her until they found the man who'd attacked her and killed the real estate broker.

He turned to Kujo. "I'm in as well."

Kujo nodded, and Gunny grinned.

"That's great news. How soon do you want to start operations?"

"Immediately, if you don't mind. I can call around and have someone set up our computer and security systems," Kujo said. "If you have any recommendations for carpenters, we can get the basement remodel started as soon as possible."

"How many of the lodge's bedrooms will you need me to set aside?" Gunny asked.

"Three would be good. One for me and one for Jake," Kujo said. "I have another recruit in mind that we might bring on sooner rather than later. And we can build another room or two into the basement as we expand our operations. Other than Jake, I don't anticipate future agents staying here. Those of us in Montana have our own homes. But getting some of the guys started, we'll need temporary living quarters for a few weeks."

"We can accommodate three rooms," Gunny turned to Jake. "I'll make sure your room has a connecting bathroom since you'll be living with us on a fulltime basis."

"I don't mind sharing the one across the hall," Jake said. "I don't want to take a prime room away from one of the lodge's customers."

Gunny's lips twisted into a wry grin. "The Brotherhood Protectors are our customers." His brow furrowed. "As far as that's concerned, do you need help moving in your belongings? Perhaps you have furniture of your own you'd prefer to have in your room."

Jake snorted. "I'll be moving out of a furnished apartment with just my clothes and a few personal items."

"That's it?" Gunny shook his head. "I guess as a Navy SEAL you didn't want to get weighed down with belongings."

"Something like that. I can collect everything in one short trip and give my landlord notice that I'm leaving."

When Jake had cleared his apartment in San Diego, he'd donated the contents to a homeless shelter, packed what he could into a duffel bag and drove to Colorado Springs where he could be close to the mountains he loved. He hadn't had a plan for what he'd do when he got there. He'd been fortunate enough to find a furnished apartment he could move right into.

And that was where he'd been for several months until Hank sent Kujo to find him.

Jake glanced toward RJ.

Her gaze met his, and he felt as if she could see right through him.

Jake looked away. "I'd like to be fully involved with the renovations," he said to Kujo.

"And you will. I'll keep you up to date on what's happening."

"Understood." Jake nodded. "My priority is Miss Tate."

"I don't want to be anyone's priority," RJ said, her mouth tightening.

"We know," Gunny cut in. "You can take care of yourself. But for now, humor your old man. Jake is your shadow. Don't make his job harder by ditching him."

She frowned. "I wouldn't purposely ditch him."

"Yeah," Gunny said. "Like you didn't ditch every nanny I hired to watch you when you were little."

"I was a child," she said. "I'm not seven years old anymore. And it was only the two nannies who smelled like old shoes."

Kujo laughed. "I would've ditched them, too."

"Since I'm stuck with a nanny, he's coming with me today on my scheduled trail ride. I have six other riders."

"Couldn't you cancel the ride?" Gunny asked. "Or I could take them. No need putting yourself out there where someone could ambush you."

"I'll be with seven other people. Safety in numbers and all that." She pushed back from the table. "Now, if you will excuse me, I'm going to get ready for a ride through the hills. I could use some fresh air and sunshine."

"In the meantime, I'll get some quotes and time estimates on the renovations," Kujo said. "And I'll have our computer guy back in Montana do some surfing on the web and see if there's anything we should be aware of concerning the murder victim."

"While you're out," Gunny said, "I could make a run into Colorado Springs for supplies."

RJ frowned. "Let me do that when we get back. I have a few things I need to pick up. Besides, it might be better to have someone here at all times since we've had a customer attacked."

Gunny's lips pressed into a thin line. "You make a good point. Should I hire some security for the bar?"

"We can perform that function for you," Kujo said. "And, as discussed yesterday, we'll have cameras installed around the premises so we can monitor who's coming and going."

"Would've been nice to have those last night," Gunny said, sighing.

"Hank has a contact in Colorado Springs," Kujo said. "His contact promised to push us to the front of the line and get us set up as soon as we settled on a location."

"Well, you have a location." Gunny clapped his hands together. "Let's get him out here."

RJ shook her head. "I liked it better when we were able to leave our doors unlocked and didn't have to worry that we might be strangled in our sleep."

Gunny's eyes narrowed. "Yeah. I liked it better when someone wasn't trying to kill my only child."

"I'll leave you men to solve the troubles of the world while I go for a ride." RJ picked up her plate and collected a few others from some of the guests before she headed for the kitchen.

Jake did the same and found her rinsing the dishes before placing them in the dishwasher. He joined her at the sink and rinsed the items he'd brought.

RJ held out her hand, taking the plates and silverware one at a time and loading them into the dishwasher. When they were finished, she wiped her hands on a towel and squared her shoulders. "Ready to ride?"

"As ready as I'll ever be," he said.

"You don't have to go, you know. I'll be with others."

"And what would happen to them if you were hurt or injured? Given our current circumstances, you might be more of a threat to your customers just by default."

Her brow furrowed. "You think?"

He shrugged. "Let's just say, it doesn't hurt to have backup." Jake poked his thumb at his chest. "I'm your backup. And I have your back. Just go with it."

She sighed. "I'm used to doing things on my own."

"Sometimes, you have to learn how to work with a partner."

"Well, partner," she tipped her head toward the refrigerator, "grab the tuna salad and jelly. We're making sandwiches for the trail."

She got out a loaf of bread and laid out over a dozen slices.

Soon, they had a variety of sandwiches, including tuna, peanut butter and jelly and deli slices of turkey. She packed them in a couple saddlebags along with two thin blankets, flasks of water and plastic cups. "Let's saddle up."

He took the saddlebags from her, slung them over his shoulder, then followed her out the door and down to the barn.

For the next hour, they brushed the horses and outfitted them with blankets, saddles and bridles.

By the time the customers gathered in the barnyard, they had the horses ready and waiting. All they had to do was adjust the stirrups to fit the legs of the riders.

Jake managed to set aside the horse he'd practiced on the night before for his own use. At least the animal would be familiar with him and hopefully cooperate.

When RJ came up to check that his girth was cinched tight enough, he asked, "This isn't your horse, is it?"

She shook her head. "No. This is Reggie. He's one of my favorites. He's got a lot of stamina and a calm personality."

"Good to know." Jake rubbed the horse's head. "Hey, Reggie. You and I are going to get along just fine."

"I usually ride Doc." RJ had selected a black and white paint gelding.

"Doc?" Jake asked.

"Short for Dr. Jekyll/Mr. Hyde." Her lips twisted into a wry grin. "Gunny named him that because he said the horse couldn't decide whether he was black or white."

"He has a sense of humor," Jake said.

RJ laughed. "A warped sense of humor." She led the animal to a post and tied him there. "I think the name fits Doc because he can't decide if he's going to be good or cantankerous." She scratched behind the horse's ears. "I like that he's a challenge. Never a dull moment with him. I don't let inexperienced riders get on him."

Jake liked that she knew the personalities of the animals in the ranch stable. She spoke of them with affection and treated them with kindness.

Once she helped the riders into their saddles, she nodded to him. "I'll open the gate. You can go ahead and mount your horse." She turned away and led her horse to the gate that opened out into one of the fields. Striker followed.

Drawing a deep breath, Jake placed his prosthetic foot into the stirrup, grabbed the saddle horn and pulled himself up into the saddle. He was the last one through the gate.

RJ nodded at him as she closed the latch.

In one smooth motion, she swung up into her saddle and trotted to the front of the line. "Ready?"

The riders all responded with excitement. The group took off at a slow, steady trot, heading across the pasture. When they came to the tree line, RJ slowed her horse to a walk and led them onto a well-worn trail, angling upward into the hills.

Jake found himself enjoying the ride. The sun shone down on the mountains, making the sky a brilliant blue. Light, fluffy clouds floated in the distance. He could easily be lulled into an idyllic stupor, if he let himself.

Instead, he used his training as a Navy SEAL to study the terrain, evaluating locations prime for an ambush or a sniper's perch.

He didn't like being at the back of the line of horses. When they stopped for lunch, he'd remedy the placement and ride close to RJ.

The woman stopped several times along the trail to point out interesting views. At one location, she had everyone look out across the valley below where a herd of elk grazed in the shadow of the aspens. At another break in the trees, she showed them a view of Pike's Peak in the distance. The majesty of the mountain held everyone in awe, including Jake. He could understand why she loved this place and being so close to nature.

The trail led down to a valley where several weathered buildings stood beside a stream. The buildings were the remains of a very small community.

RJ dismounted and helped the others by holding their horses' heads as they dismounted.

Fortunately, Jake had no trouble getting down from his horse.

When everyone was on the ground, RJ waved a hand toward the dilapidated structures. "This is Stephensville. It was an old mining community back when these hills were filled with miners seeking their fortunes in gold. Eventually, the veins played out, and the mining companies abandoned the area, leaving little ghost towns scattered among the hills. You're welcome to explore while I lay out the picnic lunch we brought. Just remember, the wood is old and rotting in some places. Be careful where you step."

The six riders, three men and three women, wandered off, entering the old houses.

RJ pulled the saddlebag off the back of her horse while Jake untied the one on his. By the time they'd laid out the blankets and pulled the sandwiches and flasks out, the guests joined them, talking excitedly about what they'd observed.

When they were finished eating, RJ pulled several flat metal pans from a saddlebag and handed them to the guests. "If you feel a hankering to pan for gold, this stream might just give you the thrill you're seeking."

The guests hurried off to strip out of their shoes and wade into the cool mountain stream.

"Anyone ever find a nugget on one of your trail rides?" Jake asked as he helped fold the blankets, pick up the trash and stash everything in the saddlebags.

RJ nodded, a smile curling her lips. "Actually, someone did find a small nugget about the size of a pencil eraser. You'd have thought he'd won the lottery."

"Where does this stream originate?"

She tipped her head toward the ground rising above them. "Somewhere up that mountain. Gunny thinks it's coming out of an old mine shaft. I think it's just a spring."

"Does Gunny own the mineral rights to this property?"

RJ nodded. "Actually, he does. Not many people own their mineral rights in Colorado. He just happened to buy the ranch from a retired Marine whose family has owned this property for over a century. He sold it because he didn't have anyone to pass it down to. And he only sold it to Gunny because he was a retired Marine."

"Has Gunny considered reopening the mine and looking for gold?"

RJ shook her head. "From what the former owner said, the vein played out in the early 1900s. His family poked around, hoping to find another vein and never did. After that, they boarded up the shaft entrances to keep people from falling into the mines."

"I imagine that's a liability for many of the ranchers around here."

RJ stared up the stream. "The mines and shafts aren't safe. A person could slide in and not be able to climb out or be trapped by collapsing walls." She nodded toward the guests panning for gold. "It's enough for people to think they just might find gold in that stream. It's one of the draws that keeps people coming back to Lost Valley Ranch. People bring their children and grandchildren to ride horses, pan for gold and play in the streams."

"You're good with the guests."

Her cheeks turned a slight shade of pink. "I like people for the most part."

"Except when they're trying to kill you," Jake added quietly.

"I have to admit, the attack was a shock. I've never been assaulted like that in all the years we've worked this ranch and the bar." She looked up at him. "I'm glad you came along when you did. I hate to think about Gunny running this place by himself."

"I'm sure he'd miss more than his worker. He loves you." Jake grinned. "Otherwise, he wouldn't have insisted I tag along with you."

"It has been kind of nice having a little help getting everything ready and cleaned up." Her brow furrowed. "Don't worry. Before long, you'll have your own business to run, and I won't be threatened by a murderer." She held up a hand. "I promise not to get used to having you around."

"Would it be such a bad thing?" He tossed the saddlebag over the back of his horse and tied the straps in place. "Having me around, that is?"

"I guess we'll find out. If everything goes according to Hank Patterson's plan, you'll be here for at least a year."

He took the other saddlebag from her and laid it across the back of her horse. "How do you feel about that?"

RJ shrugged. "We could use the steady income."

Jake shook his head. "You don't strike me as someone who hedges or avoids a difficult subject." He crossed his arms over his chest. "How do you feel about having me around for a year?"

RJ glanced at the people panning for gold. "To tell the truth, it scares the crap out of me."

Jake hadn't expected to hear her say that. "Why?"

"I don't know." RJ fumbled with the straps from the saddlebag to the saddle.

He closed the distance between them and brushed her hands aside to tie the straps himself. When he was done, he laid his hands on her shoulders and turned her to face him.

She placed her hands on his chest but didn't push him away.

"Was it the kiss?" He held his breath, waiting for her answer.

She looked everywhere but into his eyes. "Of course not."

"Really?" He touched a finger to her chin, tipping her head upward.

"Don't think you're all that," she warned, her voice breathy.

"Oh, trust me, I don't," he said. "But I have to admit, I am looking forward to getting to know you even better."

Her chin tilted higher. "As long as you keep your hands to yourself, we'll be all right."

"Does that rule go both ways?" He captured her fingers in his grip and raised them to his lips where he deposited a featherlight kiss.

She stared at his mouth on her hands, her mouth forming a small O, her breathing coming in shallow gasps.

At that moment, all Jake could think about was kissing the woman. His head lowered until his mouth hovered over hers. "Are you sure it wasn't the kiss?"

Her gaze shifted from his lips to his eyes. She opened her mouth to respond.

Bang!

The sharp report of gunfire broke the spell.

"Get down!" Jake yelled. He grabbed RJ and dragged her to the ground. "Stay down," he said.

"That was gunfire," she said. "Was someone shooting at us?"

"I'm not willing to stand around and find out."

"It's not hunting season. No one should be shooting on this property."

"Exactly." Jake glanced around at the hills surrounding them.

RJ struggled to rise. "The guests—"

"I'll take care of them. First, we have to get you behind some cover." He wrapped his arm around her, shielding her body with his. Glancing around, he spotted a fallen tree. "When I say run, get up and move with me."

Another shot was fired, spewing dirt up at their feet.

They were in the open, exposed. Targets.

"Ready?"

"Yes," she said.

His arm tightened around her, he staggered to a hunched over position and pulled her up with him. "Run!"

CHAPTER 7

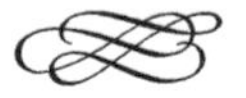

RJ RAN WITH JAKE.

When they reached a large fallen tree, he helped her over the trunk then dropped onto the other side with her.

"I can't hide while my guests are exposed." RJ started to rise.

Jake laid a hand on her shoulder. "I'll take care of them. But I can't do that if you're up and presenting yourself as a target." He gripped her arms. "Can I trust you to stay put?"

She fought the urge to run to the stream and warn the group to get down. "I'll stay put. But hurry."

"Keep your head low," he ordered.

"Be careful," she whispered.

Jake rolled over the big trunk and landed clumsily on his feet. Once he was steady, he raced for the stream and the guests who were huddled close to the banks, dragging on their shoes, their pans lying forgotten on the dirt.

"Is someone shooting at us?" a man asked, his wife held close in the circle of his arms, shaking.

"I don't know." Jake took stock of the group. They were lying low, the trees and the stream banks providing sufficient cover. The horses were tied nearby.

Another shot rang out, echoing against the hillsides, making it difficult to ascertain from which direction it was coming.

Jake studied the terrain, searching for the best location for a sniper to set up shop. From the direction the round had spewed dust, he guessed the shooter was uphill, somewhere near the origin of the stream.

"Stay down. I'm going to find out who's shooting." He left the group of men and women and followed the shadow of the trees to where the horses were tied.

Jake found Reggie. The horse shifted nervously from hoof to hoof. He whinnied when Jake slipped up beside him. After he untied the reins, he slid his prosthetic foot into the stirrup and pulled himself up into the saddle.

Hunkering low over the horse's neck, he wove between the trees, heading up the hill, following the stream.

As he reached an open, rocky area, he heard the sound of an engine revving.

Nudging his horse forward, he topped the rise.

A four-wheeler spun in a circle, kicking up dust before it shot away from Jake and Reggie.

"Go!" Jake yelled and dug his heels into the horse's flanks.

Reggie leaped forward, racing after the man on the ATV.

Jake leaned low over the animal's neck as Reggie stretched his legs, galloping after the ATV rider as he wove in and out of rocky outcroppings and trees. The trail he was on pitched downward sharply.

The ATV handled the terrain, bumping across the rocky path with ease.

Reggie slowed, his shod hooves sliding on the rocks. He picked his way down the hill. The distance between the ATV and Jake grew.

It occurred to Jake the man he was chasing could be leading him away from RJ. He could circle back to attack her as she lay unprotected. Or the man could be working with someone else who could, at the moment, be closing in on RJ.

Jake pulled back on the reins, turned the horse and raced in the opposite direction, praying he was wrong, and that RJ was safe hiding behind the fallen tree.

As he dropped down over the ridge and followed the trail back to where the others lay waiting for his return, his pulse pounded, and his heart squeezed hard in his chest.

He'd been too far away from RJ for too long.

Anything could've happened. Fortunately, she had a handgun. She could defend herself.

The sound of gunfire blasted close by, coming from the direction of the stream where he'd left RJ.

His breath caught and held as he brought Reggie to a halt near a large tree on the edge of the clearing where they'd eaten lunch. "RJ?" he called out.

The short few seconds he had to wait for her response made him lose several years off his life through worry.

"I'm here." RJ rose from the other side of the downed tree trunk.

"Are you okay?" Jake asked.

"I am, but I can't say the same for the rattlesnake I killed." She lifted her hand. The tail of a rattlesnake was pinched between her fingers.

Jake cursed.

"Did you see him?" RJ asked. "Did you see who was shooting at us?"

"Yes and no," he responded. "He was on an ATV headed away from me when I got within sight of him. The vehicle was faster than my horse. He got away without me seeing who it was. Plus, he was wearing a helmet."

"Could you identify the ATV?" RJ dropped the snake, wiped her hands on her jeans and tucked her handgun in the holster beneath her leather jacket. "Model, color?"

Jake shook his head. "He was too far away." His

lips turned up on the corners. "Nice shot. Not everyone can hit a snake with a pistol."

"It was him or me," she said. "I chose me." She drew in a deep breath. "Let's get everyone back to the barn."

The guests were shaken and ready to head back to the safety of the lodge.

"Well, we wanted a real Wild West experience," one gentleman commented as he mounted his horse.

"I could've done without the gunfight at the OK Corral," his wife muttered.

"I'm so sorry," RJ said. "We don't normally have these kinds of things happen on the ranch. The best we can do at this point is to get back to the lodge and report this incident to the sheriff."

"You're right," another man said. "It might've been a hunter, firing at an elk."

"It's not hunting season," the first man commented. "Which means, he was hunting illegally."

Jake dismounted and joined RJ beside the string of horses.

RJ and Jake assisted the guests in mounting their animals.

When they were all in their saddles, Jake got back up on Reggie, and RJ swung up onto Doc. She led the way back along the trail to the lodge.

As much as he wanted to be beside RJ, Jake knew she'd want him to help protect the guests by bringing up the rear.

He kept his eyes open and listened for the sound of an ATV all the way back to the lodge.

By the time they reached the barn, the tension was wearing on him.

Striker was in the barnyard, waiting for RJ's return.

She dismounted and scratched behind the dog's ears. "Good boy."

The guests helped remove their saddles and carry them into the tack room.

"I'm going up to the lodge to call the sheriff," RJ said. "Think you can handle the horses until I can get back?"

"I'd prefer to go with you." Jake's glance swept the area around the exterior of the barn. "That guy could have circled around and made it back here before us."

"I'll move fast," RJ said. "I want the sheriff to know what happened out here. He might want someone to come out and investigate. Could you lead a deputy up to the point where you saw the shooter?"

Jake nodded. "I think so."

"I'll hurry back."

"I'm not worried about me and the guests," Jake said. "I'm worried about someone taking another potshot at you."

She gave him a brief smile. "I appreciate that. But the sooner I call, the better." She didn't stand around and argue. Instead, she handed him the bridle and hustled up to the lodge.

Jake stood near the barn, watching until RJ entered the building.

A minute later, Gunny came out to help.

Jake was leading one of the horses out to the pasture when he saw Gunny coming across the yard.

"I'll get the gate," Gunny said and rushed forward to open the gate.

Jake led the mare through and unclipped the lead from her halter. The mare kicked up her heels and ran around the pasture before she settled down to graze.

Jake exited the pasture, Gunny latched the gate and they walked back into the barn.

"There's some snacks on the buffet in the dining room," Gunny announced to the group. "We'll take care of the rest of the horses."

The men and women left the barn, chatting among themselves as they headed for the lodge and the promise of snacks waiting for them there.

"RJ told me about the shooting," Gunny said as he brushed a roan gelding.

Jake's jaw hardened. "It could've ended so much worse than it did."

Gunner's lips thinned into a tight line. "We've never had this kind of trouble on the ranch before. I wouldn't be surprised if the guests left, afraid to be here. What with the death behind the bar and now a shooting on the trail…" The older man shook his head. "It's just not safe to be here. And now, we've put the patrons at risk. Maybe I should shut this place down until things settle."

"It's an option," Jake agreed. "I doubt your daughter would feel the same."

"She wouldn't want one of our guests to become collateral damage if someone is gunning for her."

By the time they'd finished brushing the horses, feeding them and turning them out to pasture, a sheriff's department SUV pulled into the barnyard.

RJ came out of the lodge to greet the man who climbed out of the vehicle.

Jake and Gunny released the last horse and hurried up to the lodge to where RJ and the sheriff stood.

RJ turned to Jake as he approached. "The sheriff would like to examine the spot where you found the man on the ATV.

"We just turned the horses out to pasture," Jake pointed out.

"We won't need the horses," RJ said. "There are ATVs in the shed beside the barn. We can take them."

"I'm coming," Gunny said.

"Me, too." Kujo joined them. "Sorry, I was on the phone with the security company. They can be out here tomorrow to install cameras."

"Good. Looks like we'll need them." RJ snorted softly. "Could've used some on the trail today."

Kujo's brow wrinkled. "I don't know about on the trail, but we can set them up around the lodge, the barn and the bar. If anyone tries to get in, we'll be able to see them. They'll also set up motion-sensor lighting at all the dark corners.

Gunny scratched his chin. "What's that going to set us back?"

Kujo smiled. "Nothing. Hank authorized it as part of the renovation budget."

Jake caught a look of relief on RJ's face. They really were financially tight, if the look on her face was anything to go by.

Gunny led them to the large metal shed next to the barn and threw open the door to reveal eight ATVs lined up inside. He and RJ climbed on two of them and backed them out of the shed. They returned to the bank of four-wheelers and brought out two more.

Gunny nodded toward the four vehicles. "Choose your poison. I'll get one more out for me."

Kujo and the deputy mounted a machine each. Jake waited for RJ to select one before he took the last one left standing. Gunny backed another vehicle out of the shed and led the way across the barnyard to the gate.

Gunny got off his ATV and opened the gate for the others.

RJ was the first through, calling out to her dog to stay. Jake followed as close as he could without running into her. He didn't like that she was out front. Not when she'd been a target on multiple occasions now.

They took the same trail back to the stream. Once

there, RJ held back, allowing Jake to take the lead to the place where he'd found the shooter.

Jake climbed the hill, glad for the four-wheeler this time. A horse could get into a lot of places, but the versatile, motorized vehicle got him there faster.

If he'd had the ATV when he'd chased after the other man, he might've caught him.

And the man might've made it back to the stream and killed RJ before Jake could find him in the woods.

No, he'd done the right thing going back to be with RJ. At the very least, she'd had a tree to take cover behind. Although sharing it with a rattlesnake hadn't been Jake's idea of keeping her safe.

So much for protecting her. He'd failed by not staying by her side. Next time, she might not be so lucky.

Jake had to up his game.

CHAPTER 8

RJ FOLLOWED Jake up the hill, her heart in her throat. What if the shooter had returned to the place he'd started firing shots? What if he was waiting for someone like Jake to come up over the rise so that he could shoot him square in the chest?

As Jake drove his ATV over the ridge and disappeared for the few seconds it took for RJ to catch up, her heart stopped, and her breath arrested in her lungs.

Then she topped the rise, and Jake came into view again, pulling to a stop on the hilltop.

The rest of the crew came to a stop near him.

Jake dismounted his ATV and stood looking out over the ridge to the valley below.

RJ joined him. The stream and the clearing were plain to see.

"A good sniper could've picked off any of us from this point," he said quietly.

"Apparently, he wasn't as good a shot as one of your guys," RJ reminded him. "Or one of us would be dead now."

Jake nodded and shifted his gaze to the ground around his feet. "There should be some bullet casings in this area. Maybe the sheriff could have the state crime lab do the ballistics on them."

They spent the next few minutes searching the area for bullet casings.

"Found one," Jake pointed at a bright gold casing on the ground.

"I'll take that." The sheriff pulled out a plastic glove, stuck his hand inside and reached for the casing. He dropped it into a small paper bag. "Do you see anything else? A candy wrapper, drink can, anything?"

RJ shook her head. "Nothing. And the ground is too dry for a good print of the tires on the ATV."

The sheriff shook his head. "There are hundreds of ATVs in these mountains. In addition to the ones outfitters rent to tourists, the locals all have ATVs to get around in the hills. Without a clear description of the vehicle, we're shooting in the dark."

"So, basically, we're still coming up with a blank concerning who wants me dead," RJ said. "Anything on the real estate broker who died behind the bar?"

The sheriff looked out over the hilltop. "We talked to the man's boss. Apparently, Henderson was in the area to talk to Marty Langley. He had a mining company approach him, wanting to buy the Elk Horn Ranch and its mineral rights."

"Marty Langley isn't going to sell," Gunny said. "That ranch has been in his family for over a hundred years. And it's tied up in trusts and conservations districts. Even if the mining company purchased it, I doubt they'd get permission to set up mining operations."

"Maybe the mining company has some clout with the people on the conservation boards," the sheriff offered. "I don't know. I left a message with Langley to see if Mr. Henderson made it out to present the company's offer before he was attacked."

"Let us know what you find out," Gunny said. "On second thoughts, I'll ask Marty himself. He's supposed to be at the Fools Gold annual jamboree on Friday night. I'll ask him then."

"Are you still going?" the sheriff asked.

"I'm on the bank committee to raise money for the local parks and recreation department. I'm supposed to kick off the celebration."

"What about you, Miss Tate?" the sheriff asked. "Will you be there?"

She nodded. "I'm playing the part of Madame LaBelle in the reenactment."

"The woman who won the duel between the gunfighter and the madame of the whore house?"

"Yes, sir." RJ gave the sheriff a narrow-eyed stare. "Don't judge. Sally Jo Landon backed out when she found out she was pregnant. I couldn't get anyone else to step in to take her part." She raised her hands. "When you're in charge of the reenactments, you do what you have to do." She wrinkled her nose in disgust. "Although how I got placed in charge of any of the activities is beyond me. I think JoJo had something to do with it."

"Well, there's nothing more we can do here," the sheriff said. "I suggest you find someone else to play the part of Madame LaBelle."

Oh, RJ had tried. "Trust me, the last thing I want to do is dress up as a madame and fight a fake duel in front of hundreds of people."

"Let's get back to the lodge," Gunny said. "We have guests to feed and a bar to open."

The group returned to the lodge, parked the ATVs in the shed and convened in front of the lodge.

"I'll get dinner started," RJ offered.

"And I'll open the bar," Gunny said.

"Do you ever take a day off?" the sheriff asked.

RJ smiled at her father. "Day off? What's that?"

"At least, let us help," Kujo said.

"I can assist RJ in the kitchen," Jake offered.

Kujo lifted his chin toward Gunny. "And I can help Gunny in the bar."

"I'll get the ballistics on this casing," the sheriff said, patting his pocket. "I'm sure there are hundreds of this kind of bullet in the area. But when we find the shooter, we'll have something to match up with his weapon. In the meantime, Miss Tate, stay low."

RJ nodded. "I'll do my best."

Jake hooked her arm. "We can start now by going inside."

She dug in her heels, bringing them both to a halt. "Are you asking or telling?"

Gunny burst out laughing. "Son, you've got a tiger by the tail in my Jules. She never was good at following orders."

RJ shot a glare at her father. "You were always throwing them at me. A girl has to stand up for herself."

"Duly noted." Jake dropped the elbow he'd hooked and swept out a hand. "Would you care to step inside and out of range of a potential sniper?"

She gave him a narrow-eyed glance. "Do I detect sarcasm?"

Jake held up his hands in surrender. "Not at all. Well, not much anyway. I would like it better if you'd get out of the open. You put everyone at risk, considering the shooter isn't that good a shot."

Her brow dipped. "You have a point. I don't like it, but your point's valid." She sighed. "Inside, it is." Turning the tables, she hooked Jake's elbow and led him through the back entrance of the lodge and into the kitchen. "I'm going to go shower and change into clean clothes before I start cooking. I feel like I have snake guts all over me."

"You smell like it, too," Jake said.

RJ swatted his arm. "You're not supposed to tell a woman she stinks."

"Hey," he said. "I call it like I see it. Or smell it, in this case." Jake wrinkled his nose, and then grinned.

His smile changed his face completely. From the sullen man who'd showed up at the Lost Valley Ranch yesterday with Kujo, to the man who'd saved her life twice in as many days, he seemed to be opening up. Maybe he'd regained some of his sense of worth since the incident that took his leg, his career and his team from him.

RJ's heart warmed at the thought. It only took her nearly dying twice to shake Jake out of his morose funk. The man might have to start an entirely new career, but he had the right training to protect others. He'd gone after her attacker, resuscitated her and moved her out of harm's way when the shooter had taken a shot at her. And he'd done it all on one good leg and a fake one.

Jake followed RJ and Striker up the stairs and paused outside the door to her room.

"I think we're okay in the house. No shooters are inside. You don't have to follow me into the shower," RJ said. As soon as the words left her mouth, a shiver of awareness rippled across her skin. An image of Jake and her standing in the shower together naked entered her mind.

"I won't follow you into the shower, unless you want me to." He winked.

RJ's heart fluttered. "That won't be necessary. I'm perfectly capable of washing my own body." Again, once the words left her mouth, images popped into her mind of Jake lathering a bar of soap and running his hands all over her.

Heat rose up RJ's neck, suffusing her cheeks. "I'll just get my things and be done in a few minutes." She turned to enter her room but an arm crossed in front of her, blocking her escape. She turned to stare up into his deep, dark eyes. "Yes?"

"I'm here to protect you, not to molest you," he said. "If you want me to join you in the shower, you'll have to ask."

His tone was deep, rich and smooth like melted chocolate, invading every pore.

She couldn't tear her gaze away from his, nor could she swallow in her suddenly dry throat. RJ ran her tongue across her parched lips.

The movement made Jake shift his gaze from her eyes to her mouth. He was so close. All he had to do was lower his head just a couple of inches and...

RJ leaned up on her toes and pressed her lips to his. Then she ducked beneath his arm, threw open her door and dove into the sanctuary of her room. As soon as she and Striker were through the door, she slammed it closed and leaned her back against the cool panel.

Her body was on fire, and her lips tingled from having touched Jake's. She pressed her hand to her mouth. "I didn't just kiss the man, did I?" she said aloud.

"Yes," his warm tones drifted through the wood panel, "you did."

Fire burned in her checks. RJ turned and locked the door between them. "Why are you lurking around outside my door?"

"Just making sure you're all right. You're not exactly acting normal."

"How do you know what's normal for me?"

He chuckled, the sound making her nerve endings explode with electricity. "I can't imagine you kissing someone you don't even like."

"Maybe I kiss all the boys," she said, pressing a hand to her lips. She wanted to kiss him again. What was wrong with her?

"I'll let you get to your shower. Leave the door unlocked, if you want me to join you." His footsteps sounded on the wood floor outside her door, heading toward his room on the other side of hers.

RJ listened as he opened his door and closed it. She could hear his muffled footsteps through their connecting wall. The man was on the other side. He could be stripping out of his clothes as she stood there, panicking over a silly kiss.

Taking a deep breath, RJ strode to her dresser, collected fresh underwear, a clean pair of jeans and the only pink rib-knit sweater she had in her wardrobe. For a moment, she considered putting it back and grabbing one of her faded blue chambray shirts that were her normal garb for working outdoors. Why would she want him to think she was dressing up for him? That would send all the wrong signals to the man.

She kicked off her boots, pulled the elastic band out of her hair, gathered her clothing and opened the door to her bedroom. "Stay," she said to Striker. The big dog lay down on the floor, content to sleep while she bathed. The hallway was blessedly empty.

RJ hurried across to the shared bathroom, entered, closed the door behind her and laid her things on the counter. She turned on the shower, letting the water heat while she stripped out of her clothes.

She'd just stepped beneath the spray when she thought about the lock on the door.

Leave the door unlocked, if you want me to join you.

She froze. Had she locked the door? RJ slid the shower curtain to the side a little and glanced toward the door. The lock button was horizontal. Which meant, it wasn't locked!

She flung the shower curtain to the side, leaped out of the bathtub and ran for the lock, sliding to a stop before she slammed into the door.

As she reached for the doorhandle lock, the knob turned slowly.

RJ threw her shoulder into the door.

"Oh, I'm sorry. I didn't think the bathroom was occupied," a female voice sounded outside the room.

Huh? RJ straightened, her pulse slowing. "That's okay. I'll only be a few minutes."

"Thanks. No hurry. I just wanted to freshen up before dinner."

"Five minutes is all I need," RJ said through the door and twisted the lock.

As she climbed back in the shower, she let the warm water wash away a strange sense of disappointment.

What had she thought would happen? Did she really think Jake would come into the bathroom because she'd left the door unlocked?

She was "the job" to him. He'd probably just been teasing her with sarcasm and had no intention of joining her in the shower.

RJ shampooed her hair, applied conditioner, soaped the snake yuck off her body and rinsed thoroughly before turning off the water and stepping out onto a cold wet floor.

After she dried off and squeezed the moisture out of her hair, she used her towel to dry the water she'd trailed across the floor in her hurry to lock the door. Once again, that feeling of disappointment washed over her.

Why would he want to join her in the shower? It was broad daylight, and anyone could knock on the door. Still that nagging feeling of having missed out on something exciting pressed against her chest. "Seriously?" she said aloud. "Get a grip."

"You always talk to yourself in the bathroom?" Jake's voice sounded on the other side of the door.

RJ jumped, letting out a little squeak. "Do you always lurk outside bathrooms?"

"Only when it's my turn for a quick shower." He knocked on the door. "Hurry up, woman."

She dressed quickly, finger-combed her hair, tossed her dirty clothes into the laundry hamper and opened the door. "Pushy much?" she said, her voice fading off when she came cheek to chest with the man who'd been on her mind throughout her shower.

He leaned close and tucked a damp strand of her hair behind her ear. "Only when the door is locked, and I can't make efficient use of a shower with a beautiful woman." He could have lowered his head just a little and claimed her lips.

RJ swayed toward him.

Jake stepped aside, his lip lifting in a quirky smile. "You have hungry guests. I'll only be a minute, and then I'll join you in the kitchen."

RJ hurried across the hallway, entered her room and finally filled her empty lungs. What was it about Jake that stole her breath away?

Nothing, she told herself. He's just a man. There had been a lot of men at the bar, at the lodge and in the town of Fool's Gold. What made him any different?

Nothing.

She was lying to herself. The man struck some kind of latent sexual drive within her body. Perhaps, all she needed was to have sex with him, and she'd get over him pretty quickly.

Holy hell. How awkward would it be to work in

the same building with him afterward? If he stuck with the job, he'd be there for at least a year. Maybe longer.

No. No. No.

She couldn't have sex with the man. It would make things too weird for the remainder of their lease.

Hell, she was assuming he'd *want* to have sex with her.

RJ ran a brush through her hair and scrunched the curls rather than trying to pull them back into her usual ponytail. So, it was damp. With guests waiting to be fed, she didn't have time to dry her hair.

She pulled on a pair of shoes, glanced at her reflection in the mirror and snorted. "Nothing to write home about." Though the pink sweater softened her otherwise tomboy look, she was certain Jake wouldn't opt to have sex with the rancher's daughter. Again, Jake was a bodyguard. RJ was just the body to be guarded, not jumped.

After a quick glance at the clock on her nightstand, she muttered a curse and hurried for the door. It was well past time to start dinner. She'd have to hurry to get it ready.

Yanking open the door, she ran out into the hallway and smacked into a naked, damp chest with enough force the impact knocked the breath from her lungs.

She planted her hands on the hard muscles and fought to breathe. Or was the fact she was pressed against his hard body what made it hard for her to remember how to draw air into her lungs?

Arms rose to steady her, trapping her in a muscular vice. The scent of aftershave filled her nostrils, making her stomach clench and heat coil low in her belly.

She knew whose chest it was she'd run into without having to look up to register his face.

Jake wore a pair of faded jeans and nothing else. "Whoa there." He gripped her hips and held her until she could right herself. "Are you okay?"

Her fingers curled into his skin, reveling in the feel of the solid wall of his chest. "Oh. Uh." RJ shook her head. "Sorry. I guess I wasn't looking where I was going."

"It's okay." Still, he didn't release her.

And she didn't back up or remove her hands from his chest. She was caught in a breathless vortex of desire she'd never experienced in her entire life. Having sex in the backseat of her boyfriend's car in high school hadn't inspired nearly the depth of longing she had for this Navy SEAL whom she barely knew.

"Are you sure you're okay?" Jake asked.

Striker nudged her from behind, reminding her that he was right there with her, whatever she decided to do.

When RJ realized how long she'd been standing there, heat rose up her neck and into her cheeks. She pushed against his muscular chest and straightened.

"I'm okay," she said, not feeling at all okay. This man more than confused her. He made her feel things she'd never felt before in her life. She didn't know how to process what was happening inside her own body.

"I just have to get my shirt and boots," he was saying. "If you want to wait, I'll walk down with you."

"No. That's not necessary. I'll see you in the kitchen." With those parting words, she turned and ran down the stairs across the great room and dining area and into the kitchen. Not until she made it to the commercial-grade gas stove did she stop to take a breath and touch a hand to her forehead. Was she running a fever? As hot as she was, she could be. And it had to be frying her mind for her to be so befuddled by one man.

Pulling the pots and pans from the cupboard, she fought to gain focus. People needed to eat. She had to come up with some food quickly.

Thankfully, there was hamburger meat thawed out in the refrigerator. She put a large pot of water on the stove and browned the hamburger meat. Soon, she had spaghetti sauce simmering and noodles cooking.

"What can I do?" Jake asked from behind her.

She jumped, schooled her expression and tipped her head toward the pantry. "There are a couple loaves of French bread in the pantry. Could you cut them, spread butter, sprinkle them with garlic salt and then put them on a pan in the oven? I've already preheated it."

"Gotcha." He found the loaves, a pan and a serrated knife and went to work on the bread. Before long, he had the bread in the oven and the scent of garlic filling the air.

Without being asked, he found plates and silverware and set the table, coming back to check the oven to keep from burning the bread.

The man was sexy and able to think for himself in a kitchen? What manner of fairytale had she stumbled into?

"Are we making a salad to go with the spaghetti?" he asked.

"Yes. The vegetables are in the fridge." RJ stirred the sauce and went to help him pull lettuce, spinach, tomatoes, banana pepper, onions and cheese from the drawers in the large refrigerator.

While RJ cut the lettuce and tomatoes, Jake handled the onions, banana peppers and cheese.

By the time the noodles and bread were done, they had individual salads on the tables where the guests would sit.

"I'll drain the noodles, if you want to find a serving dish for the spaghetti sauce," Jake offered. He carried the pot of noodles to the sink and poured them into a strainer.

RJ placed a large ceramic bowl beside him. "For the noodles." Once he poured the noodles into the bowl, she placed a pasta spoon inside it and made quick work of ladling portions of noodles into pasta bowls.

Jake followed with spoons full of sauce.

They carried the bowls to the tables.

The guests seated themselves and dug into the salads while Jake and RJ brought out baskets of garlic bread for the tables and glasses of water, tea and sodas, based on what the individuals requested.

When all of the guests had been served, RJ carried the large serving bowl of noodles and a big bowl of salad out to the table reserved for lodge staff. Jake brought the sauce and a basket of garlic bread.

Kujo and Gunny appeared and helped by bringing out glasses of water and iced tea.

"Who's running the bar?" RJ asked.

"JoJo's got everything under control," Gunny said. "She insisted we come eat dinner—as long as we bring her a plate of food when we're done."

"Deal," RJ said. "Have a seat and eat while it's still hot."

Soon, they had all loaded their dishes and dug into the food.

RJ was amazed at how quickly they'd been able to prepare a full meal for everyone.

"This is great," Gunny said. "Thank you, Jules, for slaving over the stove."

"I couldn't have done it without Jake's help," she admitted.

"I think this arrangement is going to work out

more in our favor," Gunny said. "We get a steady income and more help."

"It works out for all of us," Jake said. "I haven't had a homecooked meal in a long time."

"And I didn't have to cook it all by myself," RJ said. Yeah, Jake was every woman's dream man. She'd have to guard her heart or risk falling in love with the man.

She couldn't let that happen when he could have any woman he crooked his finger at. One who actually knew how to wear a dress and liked doing it.

RJ stole a glance across the table at Jake. His gaze met hers, and a smile curled the corners of his lips.

Damn. Could the man read minds, too? Did he know she was thinking about falling in love with him?

Her cheeks burned as she turned away from his all-knowing stare.

RJ needed to get a grip on her emotions where Jake Cogburn was concerned. And she needed to do so before she really did fall in love with the man.

CHAPTER 9

All the time Jake had spent in his apartment in Colorado Springs, he'd grieved the leg he'd lost and hesitated leaving his cave to figure out life as he now had to live it—one leg short of a pair.

In the past twenty-four hours, he'd proven to himself that his life wasn't over. Not only could he get around on foot, but he could also ride a horse and...kiss a girl.

Maybe life after the Navy SEALs wouldn't be as bad as he'd originally thought.

Being on Lost Valley Ranch, getting out in the open and experiencing nature had breathed new purpose into him.

And RJ...

The woman never stopped. She'd almost been smothered to death and had been shot at, and all she could think about was taking care of her guests.

She didn't seem to realize just how sexy she

was. Having grown up with a Marine gunnery sergeant father, she hadn't had the luxury of a mother to show her by example how to be a lady.

Hell, she was more of a lady than some of the women Jake had dated. She was tough, caring and had a body that didn't quit. And her lips were soft and incredibly kissable.

They finished dinner quickly, speaking sparingly. Gunny wanted to get back to the bar before it got too busy for JoJo to handle on her own.

"I'll be over as soon as I clean up the kitchen," RJ promised.

"I'll help Gunny," Kujo offered. "I'm not sure about mixed drinks, but I can serve beer."

"You're on," Gunny said as they headed out the door, carrying a plate of food for JoJo.

The guests finished their meals and helped clear their tables.

"I'll wash," Jake said. "You can dry, since you know where everything goes."

"Sounds like a good plan," RJ said.

Jake filled the sink with hot sudsy water and quickly washed the dishes. Their hands touched every time he passed a dish to RJ to dry. A spark of electricity passed up his arm each time.

When the last dish was dried and put away, Jake emptied the sink and rinsed it clean.

"Thank you," RJ said. "Things go a lot faster with help."

"Should we go to the bar and see if Gunny and Kujo need help?"

RJ nodded. "Let me set up the coffee and cocoa bar for the guests to help themselves. Once they're happy, I'll be ready to go over."

"I'll help." Jake carried an urn of hot water into the dining room and laid it on a buffet cabinet against the wall.

RJ arranged a tray of ceramic mugs and packets of tea, cocoa and instant coffee for the guests. "Help yourselves," she invited the guests. "We'll be at the Watering Hole if you want something a little stronger."

RJ pulled on a jacket. "You might want to wear something a little warmer. The night is supposed to get down into the thirties."

"I'll be fine for the short walk between the lodge and the bar." He held the door for her.

As they stepped out of the lodge into the cool of the night, he inhaled the mountain air, enjoying the beauty of the stars above and the woman walking beside him in companionable silence.

They hadn't gone twenty yards from the lodge when a loud boom sounded and shook the ground beneath their feet.

Striker yelped and dropped to his belly, shaking.

RJ held onto Jake as he ducked toward the ground. "What the hell?"

"Sounded like a mortar round," Jake said.

RJ reached for Striker and wrapped her arms

around his neck. "It's okay, boy. It's okay." The animal didn't like loud noises. After having been in an explosion himself, he was sensitive to fireworks, gunshots and mortar rounds. She coaxed him to his feet and kept a hand on his neck as they hurried toward the bar.

Gunny, JoJo and Kujo came out the back door of the bar as they neared.

"Did you hear that?" RJ asked.

"Not only did we hear it," Gunny said. "It rattled the glassware."

"What do you suppose it was?" JoJo asked.

"If it were in the winter, I'd say it sounded like avalanche control mortar rounds," Gunny said. "But, right now, there isn't that much snow in the mountains for them to worry about avalanches." He turned to the bar. "I'll call the sheriff and ask if they've had other reports."

They all entered the bar.

Striker took his position on the dog bed RJ had placed behind the bar.

Patrons gathered around their tables, all talking at once. One man looked up. "What was it?"

Gunny shrugged. "Not sure." He lifted the phone on the counter and called the sheriff. After a few minutes on the phone, he hung up and shook his head. "They heard it in Fool's Gold as well," Gunny said. "The sheriff thinks it might be someone operating illegally in one of the old mines."

RJ frowned. "Dynamite?"

Gunny nodded.

"Isn't dynamite a controlled substance? Can't they chase down everyone in the area who has access to it?" RJ asked.

Gunny nodded. "It's possible. The sheriff said he'd look into it. But it'll take time."

"Wonderful." RJ's lips pressed together. "In the meantime, we might have explosions going off in any number of mine shafts sprinkled across the county."

"That's about the extent of it." Gunny touched RJ's arm. "Why don't you call it a night? I can close up the bar. You've had a helluva a day."

"I'm fine," she argued, though the thought of going to bed early did appeal to her.

Gunny crossed his arms over his chest and gave RJ a narrow-eyed stare. "Do you always have to disagree with me?"

RJ smiled. "No, sir. And if you insist I call it a night, I insist you sleep in come morning. I can handle breakfast."

Gunny shook his head. "You feed the animals. No. I'll make breakfast as usual."

She crossed her arms over her chest just like her father. "Then I'll stay and help clean up at closing."

"RJ, you're as stubborn as your father." JoJo slapped an empty tray on the bar. "I can close up the bar, and you both can call it a night."

RJ and Gunny turned to JoJo.

"No way," RJ said at the same time as Gunny said. "No."

JoJo planted a fist on one hip. "Seriously? You two are too much alike." She took a loaded tray and headed back to a table full of thirsty men.

"Okay," RJ said. "I'll call it a night. But you have to sleep in at least an extra hour. I'll get breakfast started after I take care of the animals."

"And I'll be there to help with the animals and breakfast," Jake said.

"Which will make it all go faster." RJ smiled. "So you see, we can take care of things while you catch up on some rest."

Gunny frowned. "Any more than six hours of sleep a night—"

"—is a waste of time." RJ shook her head. "And you wonder where I get that philosophy." She turned to Jake. "I'm headed to the lodge."

"Come with me to my car, first," JoJo said. "I have your dress for the reenactment. Sally Jo Landon asked me to give it to you. You might have to safety pin it in places to make it fit you right. I think you have a smaller waist and hips than she does."

"And everything else," RJ muttered. She didn't want to play the part of a madame. Hell, she didn't know how to put on a corset, much less a dress with several petticoats. She sure as hell didn't have the cleavage to pull off being a madame. "JoJo, are you sure you don't want to play the part of the madame? I'd pay you a premium to do it."

JoJo held up her hands. "No. I'm working the funnel cake booth."

"How did you get a funnel cake booth, and I'm stuck as a madame?"

"A madame who shoots a gunslinger." JoJo set another tray filled with empty mugs and bottles on the counter. "You'd make a much more convincing madame than I would."

"Are you kidding? You're cute and pretty badass," RJ said.

"And I'm too short for the dress." She held her hands out to the side, palms up. "Unless we want to come up with an entirely new costume, we have to go with whoever will fit in the dress."

RJ cursed."Fine. Let's get the dress." She looked around for Jake. He was only a few steps away, apparently watching her every move. When she started for the exit, Striker surged to his feet and trotted alongside her. Jake pushed away from the wall and followed her out.

JoJo was first to the door, about to lead the way out the back. Before she could take a step through the exit, Jake blocked her path. "Stay here until I clear the area."

JoJo glanced at RJ, her brows raised.

Jake left the building, closing the door behind him. A minute later, he was back. "All clear as far as I can tell. But you need to stay close to me."

"Gladly," JoJo said with a wink. She stood on one side of RJ, Jake had the other, effectively sandwiching RJ between them.

As they walked out to JoJo's car, Striker following behind.

"Sally Jo had it dry cleaned, so you're good to go for the Friday night shootout." JoJo opened the truck and pulled out the dress wrapped in plastic from the drycleaners. She held it up and grinned.

RJ groaned. The dress was cut regrettably low in the front, and the corset would push things up in all the wrong places. Or right places, depending on who cared. The men might enjoy seeing her cleavage on display. Well, what there was to display?

Who was she kidding? "I can't do this."

"You can, and you will," JoJo said. "Madame LaBelle was such a huge part of Fool's Gold back in the day. You can't let everyone down."

Jake's brow wrinkled. "What's this about a shootout on Friday night?"

"Madame LaBelle was one of the original residents of Fool's Gold. She got tired of the local gang stirring up trouble for the miners, so she had a shootout with the gang's leader. No one thought she even knew how to fire a revolver, much less hit anything." JoJo laughed. "She showed them when she killed the leader and threatened to shoot any of his followers if they bothered the miners ever again."

"And you're playing the part of her shooting the gang's leader?" Jake frowned. "Not sure I like the idea of you being exposed to a crowd of people."

RJ snorted. "Exposed being the keyword."

"Someone tried to shoot you today," Jake reminded her. "What's to keep him from trying again? And in a townful of people, he could easily get lost in a crowd."

"All the more reason for me to call off the annual shootout," RJ said, "besides the fact there would be guns involved."

"They use cap guns," JoJo said. "But maybe you're right. It might put you out there where someone could hurt you. We can find someone else to play the madame. Although who that might be, I don't know at this late date."

RJ held the dress back from JoJo. "No. I'll do it. I'm the one scheduled. If I put someone else in the dress, whoever took a shot at me might shoot my replacement, thinking it's me." She shook her head. "I'd feel awful if someone took a bullet for me."

"I'd feel awful if *you* took a bullet," JoJo said. "I think we need to call this entire event off and just skip right to the Sadie Hawkins dance."

RJ groaned. "Do I have to go?"

JoJo frowned. "You promised the mayor you'd be there. You're representing Lost Valley Ranch. Gunny paid for the advertisement."

They no longer desperately needed the business. Not when they had Hank Patterson's rent money about to come in steadily to meet the usual bills. But it would be nice to have paying guests in order to make some much-needed improvements to the lodge and barn. Still…dances weren't RJ's thing, though she loved to two-step.

"You don't have a date for the Sadie Hawkins dance, do you?" JoJo shook her head. "I could get one of my cousins…"

"No." RJ shook her head. "I really don't feel like going."

"You have to. You promised." JoJo turned to Jake. "Take Jake. If he's supposed to be your bodyguard, it makes sense to take him. And that way, people don't have to know he's your bodyguard. He could just be your date. For that matter, you two can pretend to be a thing until we find the bastard who's terrorizing you. No one will be the wiser, and it'll look natural that he's always with you."

RJ shook her head. "Jake doesn't want to go to the Sadie Hawkins dance any more than *I* want to."

"Excuse me." Jake held up a hand. "Do I have a say in this matter?"

"Yes," JoJo said at the same time RJ said, "No."

"If you need to be at the Sadie Hawkins dance, I can take you." He drew in a deep breath. "I have to warn you, I haven't danced since—" he paused, frowned and finished with, "—in a while."

"Since you lost your leg?" JoJo asked.

"JoJo!" RJ glared at her friend.

"What?" JoJo looked from RJ to Jake and back. "You didn't know?" She gave RJ a crooked grin. "I'm sure Jake knows."

Jake's jaw tightened.

RJ was mortified her friend had outed Jake before he was ready to reveal his injury for himself.

"You knew?" Jake asked quietly.

RJ's cheeks heated. She nodded.

"How? When?"

"I saw you practicing mounting Reggie in the barn." She shrugged. "It was pretty obvious."

"You two want me to leave you alone to talk about this?" JoJo asked. "I'm sorry. I thought everyone knew."

"How did *you* know?" RJ asked. "Did Jake tell you?" She glanced at Jake and back to JoJo.

JoJo shook her head. "I have a friend who lost his leg in an IED explosion when we were deployed to Afghanistan. He walked with a limp like Jake's. I assumed he had a similar situation." She grimaced. "I hope I didn't speak out of turn. You seem to have adjusted well. My friend is already planning to run his first half-marathon on his prosthesis. I think that's pretty amazing. A dance will be a piece of cake for a guy like you."

"Thanks, JoJo. I'll take the dress and make a decision later as to whether to cancel the Madame LaBelle shootout. And I will be at the Sadie Hawkins dance as promised." She met Jake's gaze. "If Jake doesn't have second thoughts about going..."

"I'm in," he said.

"We'll walk you back inside, and then I'm calling it a night," RJ said.

"Oh, good." JoJo clapped her hands. "Now, I just have to find a date for the dance."

RJ huffed. "And you were giving me grief."

JoJo grinned and walked toward the bar. "It worked, didn't it? Maybe Emily can be my date if we can't find fellas to go with us."

"You work on that," RJ said, opening the back door for JoJo. "You're cutting it a little close, aren't you? We only have a few days."

"I'm not worried about it." JoJo turned in the threshold of the door. "I'm just glad you're getting out. You spend too much time on the ranch. You know there's a whole world out there you're missing out on."

"I'm happy on the ranch," RJ insisted.

"Yeah," JoJo said, her tone indicating she was not at all convinced. "You better bone up on your dancing skills. It's been a while since the last time you hit the dance floor."

"Don't worry about me." RJ hugged JoJo. "You're the one who has to find a date."

JoJo entered the bar and closed the door, leaving RJ and Jake alone outside.

Striker lay on the ground nearby, relaxed, but alert.

"You know you don't have to take me to the Sadie Hawkins dance if you don't want to," RJ said.

"I wouldn't have offered if I didn't intend to go." Jake's voice was tight, his gaze on the night surrounding them.

RJ shot a glance in Jake's direction. She remembered how he'd practiced mounting a horse before he'd gone riding the following day. He was probably hesitant to dance at this point. "Okay, but just because we're going to a dance doesn't mean you have to dance."

"If you want to dance, I'll dance," he said stiffly.

"I could use some practice," she said softly. "Gunny made sure I knew how to two-step. But that's all I know, and it's been a while since I danced standing on his feet. Do you know how to two-step?"

Jake nodded. "It's not that hard to remember," he said. "It's a simple quick, quick, slow, slow movement."

RJ knew that. Gunny had drummed it into her as a child. He'd told her that he'd fallen in love with her mother at a country-western bar, dancing to the two-step.

RJ had dreamed of falling in love with a man on the dance floor like her mother and father had. But that just hadn't happened. The ranch kept her too busy to think about dancing, except for the once or twice a year there were festivals and events JoJo or Emily dragged her to.

Again, she knew the steps, and based on what Jake had just said, he did, too. But did he know how to dance them now that he was working with a prosthetic leg?

"Could you show me?" RJ asked. "Sounds simple, but I'm sure it's not as easy to music. We have a sound system in the great room."

"I'm sure you'll remember as soon as you're at the

Sadie Hawkins dance. You can watch others before we have to get out there."

"I'd rather not experiment in public, if you don't mind," RJ insisted. "Again, we don't have to dance if you don't want to."

"We're dancing," Jake said, his tone firm.

"Okay." RJ stopped halfway to the lodge and stood in the moonlight. "Wanna start here? In the dark, where no one can see us?"

She'd picked a level spot on the ground to make it easier on Jake since he could only feel one of his feet.

RJ held up her hands.

Jake took her in his arms.

She rested one palm on his shoulder and the other in his hand. Their closeness set off all kinds of fireworks inside her. She chalked it up to nerves. Nothing else.

"Remember," he said. "Quick, quick, slow, slow." He leaned into her and stepped forward on his prosthetic foot, crushing her toes beneath his.

RJ bit down on her bottom lip to keep from crying out. But she did hop a little. "My fault. I wasn't ready."

He stopped, his brow furrowing. "You're right. Maybe we should show up and not dance."

When he tried to release her hand, she held firm.

"No," RJ said. "I'm committed to dancing. JoJo will never let me live it down if I don't."

"Then maybe you should ask someone else. It is a

Sadie Hawkins dance. You get to choose your partner."

"You asked *me*," RJ reminded him.

"Exactly. You didn't ask me, as is the custom."

"Is that all I have to do?" RJ smiled up at him. "I don't guarantee to be the prettiest girl at the ball, but will you go with me to the Sadie Hawkins Dance?"

For a long moment, Jake stared downward.

RJ met his gaze, falling into the darkness of his eyes. For a moment, she thought he'd refuse her offer.

Jake sighed. "I can't guarantee I'll get the dancing right, but I'll do my best not to cripple you by stepping on your feet."

RJ grinned. "Deal. Now, let's try this again. I don't want to embarrass myself in front of all the people I know in the county."

"I hope I won't embarrass you." Jake held her hand and cupped her back with the other. "Ready this time?"

She nodded.

When he stepped out this time, she moved her foot back at the same time. Soon, they were moving around the yard together.

When Jake finally brought her to a stop, they were close to the lodge. "We'd better go in. It's getting late."

"Yeah. It is." She dropped her hand from his shoulder, but when she started to let go of his hand, he held on.

RJ turned and fell in step beside him, holding his

hand all the way up the front porch steps. "Could we practice with music tomorrow night?"

Jake stopped in front of the door. "That's a good idea."

"Maybe if we practice every night until Friday, we'll have it down."

He lifted her hand to his lips. "I know what you're doing."

She stared at his lips on her hand, willing him to kiss her skin. "What do you mean?"

"I don't want to be anyone's pity date," he said, his lips thinning.

RJ's gaze shot to his. "Oh, believe me. If anyone is a pity date, it's me. I don't have a clue how to date. I'm more comfortable in jeans and boots than a dress. And Lord help me if I have to wear heels. I'm likely to break an ankle. So, if there's any pitying to be had, it's on me."

He shook his head slowly. "You have no idea how desirable you are, do you?"

"Me?" she squeaked.

Jake kissed the backs of her knuckles then pulled her into his arms. "Yes, you. I've wanted to kiss you since I stepped on your toe and you made it sound like it was your fault. You have a big heart, and you care about people. That's sexier than any fancy dress or hairdo."

RJ raised a hand to her ponytail. "I don't even know how to do my hair."

"Don't change a thing about you. You're perfect

the way you are." Then he kissed her.

RJ leaned into him, her hands resting on his chest, her lips forming to his, opening to accept his tongue. She wanted the kiss to go on forever. Being close to him wasn't nearly close enough. She wanted to feel his body against hers, to touch him skin to skin.

Heat coiled low in her belly and spread outward to the very tips of her fingers.

And then the kiss was over.

Jake stepped back, his chest rising and falling as if he'd been running.

RJ finally remembered how to breathe and drew in a deep, shaky breath. "Wow."

"Go to bed, Rucker Juliet Tate."

She blinked up at him, trying to focus on his words. "What?"

"Go now," he said, his voice harsh. "Before I do something else I might regret."

She moved forward. "What if I want you to do that something?"

He pushed his hand through his hair, standing it on end. "Go. To. Bed."

His face was set in firm lines. His jaw so tight it twitched.

"Okay. But just so you know…there were two people participating in that kiss. And I, for one, liked it." She turned and rushed into the lodge, afraid she'd throw herself at him if she stood in front of him much longer.

"RJ?" Jake called out after her.

She stopped. Had he changed his mind?

"Are you forgetting someone?" Jake held the door open and Striker trotted in.

"Oh, baby." She bent to scratch him behind his ears, then straightened, her gaze meeting Jake's. "Thanks."

Then she turned and walked away, Striker following.

From all indications, Jake had enjoyed the kiss as much as RJ had. Why had he gone cold so quickly?

When she heard the door to the lodge close behind her, RJ glanced over her shoulder.

Jake must have gone back out.

She took that opportunity to run up the stairs and into her bedroom, closing the door softly behind her and Striker. Once in the sanctuary of her room, she pressed her fingers to her swollen lips, the tingling continuing long after the kiss had ended.

What was wrong with her? She'd never felt so close to throwing herself at a man. A man she barely knew.

Striker whined beside her.

RJ rested her hand on his head. "It's okay, boy." She wasn't so sure it was okay, but Striker needed the comfort. Hell, she could have used some reassurance herself.

Was it possible to fall for someone so quickly after meeting him? Was that it? Was she falling in love with the Navy SEAL?

Lord help her if she was.

CHAPTER 10

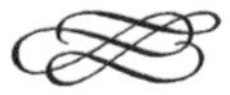

JAKE WENT to bed that night confused.

Confused.

Just like RJ had stated the first time he'd kissed her.

He laid awake for a good portion of the night, trying to make sense of what he was feeling. Every time he kissed RJ, it wasn't enough. He wanted more.

Why? Was he wishing he was his old self and trying to make up for the fact he wasn't? Was he really falling for the rancher's daughter, who was such a good shot she'd nailed a rattlesnake with a handgun?

For the rest of the week he made a promise to himself to take a step back. To stop kissing RJ. He'd focus on finding the guy who'd killed the realtor and tried to choke the life out of the amazing Tate woman. That would be a better use of his time than throwing himself at the female rancher whose lips melted him all the way to his core.

The next morning, after he helped RJ with the chores in the barn, Jake met with Kujo.

RJ was busy making breakfast with Gunny in the kitchen.

"Has Hank learned anything more about Robert Henderson or the mining company he represented?"

"As a matter of fact, he did." Kujo opened his laptop on a table in the dining room, brought up an internet browser then keyed in "Omega Mining Corporation."

"This is the mining company that wanted Mr. Henderson to make an offer for the Elk Horn Ranch. The CEO is a Frank Barnes," Kujo said. "I've left a message with his secretary, hoping to schedule a meeting with him today. Do you want to come?"

"Yes, we do," RJ answered from behind them. She carried a tray of danishes and biscuits to the buffet against the wall. "I'd like to know what their plans were."

"I'll let you know what I find out as soon as I hear something from Barnes," Kujo said.

"Anything else?" Jake asked.

Kujo shook his head. "No." His frown lightened. "But Molly said the baby's kicking like a linebacker." Kujo grinned.

"I bet you're anxious to get back to her," Jake said. He couldn't imagine being that far away from his pregnant wife. The sooner they got things rolling on the new office of the Brotherhood Protectors, the sooner Kujo could get back to Montana.

"She's doing well, and Swede's wife, Allie is looking out for her." Kujo brought up another screen with a spreadsheet on it. "These are the tasks we need to accomplish to get things rolling on the new office. I've already contacted a contractor to get the renovations started in the basement. He'll start next Monday. He projected four weeks to make the changes."

"That's fast," Jake said, impressed.

"He's an old friend of Hank's from their military days. They'll throw everything at it to get it done on time." Kujo pointed to the next item on the list. "Our communications team will arrive later today to install the internet and security systems."

"It'll be good to have the security system in place," Jake said. "Hopefully, that will deter anyone from attacking the Tates or their guests."

Kujo nodded. "Until the renovations in the basement are complete, we'll set up the monitors in Gunny's office, here in the lodge."

Kujo's cellphone buzzed. He glanced at the caller ID. "Good. It's from Barnes's office." He answered. "Yes, this is Joseph Kuntz. One o'clock? Yes, ma'am. We'll be there. Thank you for getting us in so quickly." After he ended the call, he glanced across at Jake. "One o'clock."

"Did you hear that?" Jake called out to RJ as she

carried a tray full of dirty coffee mugs through the kitchen's swinging door.

"One o'clock. I'm going with you." The door swung closed behind her, and then opened again for Gunny, who carried in a bucket of water. He primed the coffee maker with a fresh filter and grounds, poured in the water and switched it on.

"In the meantime, we might want to pay a visit to Marty Langley at the Elk Horn Ranch," Jake said.

Gunny set the urn on the bar. "I'll give him a call before we go, and then go with you. He's a cantankerous son of a bitch, more prone to shoot first and ask questions later."

"Good to know," Kujo said.

"One of us needs to stay at the ranch to take care of our guests," RJ said. She didn't add, but Jake could guess, that she wanted someone there to look out for their safety.

"I'll go with Kujo to speak to Marty," Gunny said. "You can go with them to Colorado Springs later to meet with the mining company CEO."

"Surely, the sheriff's department or state police are investigating both," RJ said. "Perhaps we should ask the sheriff."

"If the state police have taken over the case, the sheriff won't necessarily be conducting the investigation," Kujo said.

"If Marty knows something, he'll let me in on it," Gunny said. "I can do that this morning. At the very least, you'll know if Marty got that offer and what he planned to tell the mining company."

"I've got a few things I need to do this morning around the barn," RJ said. "I'll be ready at noon to go to Colorado Springs."

After the guests were fed and the dishes done, Kujo and Gunny set off for a meeting with Marty Lange.

Jake followed RJ and Striker out to the barn, schooling himself to be vigilant and hands-off with RJ.

Inside the barn, RJ picked up a hay rake and went to work mucking the first stall, shoveling soiled straw into a wheelbarrow.

Jake grabbed another rake and wheelbarrow and mucked the second stall, smiling as he went. Nothing said sexy like a woman up to her elbows in horse shit. Under those conditions, keeping his hands off her would be easier than he'd thought.

They worked through one side of the barn and then the other, emptying their wheelbarrows in a pile behind the barn. When they were finished, they spread fresh straw on the floors of the stalls, cleaned the wheelbarrows and rakes and filled the water troughs in the pastures.

Striker stood guard throughout from his perch on a short stack of hay bales.

By the time they hung the rakes on the wall, Jake had worked up a sweat and smelled like horse dung.

The work had been hard, but it felt good to see the results in clean stalls ready for horses to occupy.

He glanced at his watch. "We have enough time to shower and grab a bite to eat. Kujo and Gunny should be back soon."

"Definitely need the shower." She gave him a brief chin lift. "Good job on mucking stalls. Thanks for helping, even though you didn't have to."

"Strangely, it felt good to work hard. I recognize some of the muscles I haven't used in a while." He flexed his arms and stretched his back. "Yup. I'll feel them tomorrow as well."

"It's not the most glamorous work, but it has to be done." RJ wiped her hands on her dirty jeans and led the way up to the lodge.

Once inside, Striker headed for his bed in front of the fireplace, plopping down for a much deserved morning nap.

RJ chuckled. "It's hard work sleeping on haystacks, isn't it?"

The sound of her laughter warmed Jake's insides. "You have a great smile. Did you know that?"

She frowned, her cheeks turning pink. "Whatever."

"Seriously, hasn't anyone ever told you that?" Jake shook his head. "If not, then you aren't smiling enough."

Her frown deepened. "I smile."

His lips twitched. "Like now?"

Her frown softened and spread into a little grin.

"Okay. Maybe I could work on that. I do find a lot to be happy about. I should express that happiness more often."

"Only if you really feel it," Jake said.

"Now look who's being all philosophical." She headed for the stairs. "I'll only be a few minutes in the shower."

"I'm in right after you." He pulled his shirt out and sniffed. "Yeah. I definitely need it."

RJ sniffed. "You and me both." She headed up the stairs.

Jake gave her a few minutes head start, and then climbed the stairs to his room where he grabbed what he needed in the way of clean clothes and his shaving kit.

Crossing the hallway to the bathroom, he turned the knob. When it opened, he was surprised the shower was still going and the room was filled with steam.

"You said to leave the door unlocked if I wanted you to join me," RJ's voice echoed against the ceramic tiles.

Jake's groin tightened.

RJ's naked body was silhouetted against the shower curtain, outlining her slim build, the swell of her hips and the soft curve of her breasts.

He wanted her more than anything or anyone he'd ever wanted in his life. Jake stepped forward, his prosthesis catching on the bathmat, reminding him what it would be like if he stepped into the shower with her. He'd have to remove his fake leg and struggle to get over the edge of the tub and into the water.

No, he couldn't. Not in front of this strong woman who could run circles around him now that he'd lost his leg.

"I'll wait until you're done," he murmured and backed toward the door.

"What? Are you afraid to show me what you've got?" She yanked the curtain back and stood before him naked. "I don't care if you only have one leg. I care that you're willing to help me do tasks most men would walk away from. I care that you don't complain when you do them. And I think you're sexy as hell when you're covered in horse manure." She planted a hand on her hip. "Now, if you're leaving because you don't find me the least bit attractive, I'll understand. But don't leave because you're afraid to show me any kind of weakness."

For a long moment, Jake stood in front of her, torn between his promise to remain hands-off and his desire to hold this amazing woman and make passionate love to her.

"You don't have any idea of how much I want to touch you," he said through gritted teeth.

"Then do it." She lifted her chin. "But hurry because I'm losing my nerve. It isn't every day, or every decade, that I make an offer like this to a man. If you take too long to make up your mind, I might lose my nerve."

"Sweet Jesus," he said, ripping the hem of his T-shirt out of the waistband of his jeans. "I've got to be out of my mind."

"If that's the case, then so am I." She stepped out onto the bathmat and helped him drag the shirt up over his head, tossing it into the laundry basket in the corner. Then her hands went to the button on his jeans, flicked it open and then slowly lowered his zipper.

His cock sprang free, and she cupped it in her hands.

She grinned. "I'm glad it's not just me."

"Not just you?" he said, barely able to push air past his vocal cords. He was so tight and hard he found it hard to breathe.

"As soon as I heard the door open and knew it was you, my pulse went ballistic, and my body seemed to be on fire. Is that how you feel?"

"Oh, baby, that and more." He pulled her into his arms and kissed her hard on the lips.

When she opened to him, he thrust his tongue past her teeth and swept it along the length of hers, loving how warm and wet she was.

Then it came time to remove his jeans and time seemed to come to a standstill.

"Don't stop now," RJ implored. "We can do this. You just have to show me how."

"I don't know how," he said. "I haven't made love to a woman since this." He waved a hand toward his leg.

"Then let's take it one step at a time." She hooked her fingers into the waistband of his jeans and shoved them down over his ass and thighs.

When she reached his knees, he gripped her arms and made her stop.

RJ glanced up at him. "Don't stop now."

"I need to sit to remove my boot."

She smiled and rose, backing him up to the counter. "Sit. I'll get the boot."

He eased his ass onto the cool counter and let her work the boot off his good foot. Once the boot was off, she looked up.

"Should I take off the other boot?"

He shook his head. "No. I'll take care of it." Jake drew in a deep breath. If taking off his leg freaked her out, he'd leave and never say another word about it.

He pushed his jeans down to his ankles, rolled the outer liner down over the prosthesis, slipped his residual limb out of the device and removed the inner liner.

He'd done it often enough, the process went quickly. When he glanced up, he prayed RJ wouldn't be appalled. Or worse, that she would pity him.

RJ held out her hand, neither smiling nor cringing. "I'll wash you, if you'll wash me."

He took her hand, braced his other hand on the wall and hopped over to the tub, sat on the rim, swung his good leg over and stood.

RJ got into the tub with him and pulled the curtain closed.

While she worked up a lather in her hands, she let Jake have the full force of the spray.

Starting at his neck, she worked her hands over his shoulders, around to his back and down his torso. When she reached his shaft, she paused. "I'm not well-versed in this. Let me know what you like or don't like. I won't be offended."

"Sweetheart, just touching me will get me off."

"Then you will probably like this." She ran her soapy hands the length of his cock and back to the base where she fondled his balls.

Jake moaned, holding onto the wall to keep his balance. When he thought he might explode, he caught her hand in one of his.

"Does that bother you?" she asked.

"More than you can imagine," he rasped.

"I'm sorry."

"Oh, sweetheart, don't be," he said with a tight laugh. "It bothers me in the best way." He took the soap from her, leaned his back against the wall, balanced on his one foot and worked up a lather in his palms. Then he pulled her close and worked the soap over her shoulders, down her arms and up her sides to cup her breasts. God, she felt good. As tough as she was in the barn and on horseback, her skin was silky smooth and warm against his fingertips.

He rolled the beads of her nipples between his

thumb and forefingers until her back arched and she pushed closer to him.

Abandoning her breasts, he smoothed his hands down her torso, one hand going to curve around her hip, the other diving low to curl into her sex.

RJ's head dropped back. Her hands came up to capture the one he'd placed between her legs.

Instead of pushing him away, she cupped his hand and urged him to go deeper.

He obliged, sinking his finger into her sex.

Her channel was slick with her juices.

Jake groaned.

RJ's head came up, and her forehead creased. "Is it too hard balancing on one foot?"

"No," he grit out. "It's too hard holding back."

"Then don't." She reached up, cupped his check. "Nothing is sexier than a man who isn't afraid to work for what he wants." And she leaned up on her toes and pressed her lips to his in a hard kiss.

With his hand, he encircled the back of her neck and deepened the kiss, pushing past her teeth to claim her tongue with his.

When he came up for air, he gave a strangled laugh. "Is that all it takes to get you hot? Good old-fashioned sweat?"

She lifted one shoulder, the shower's spray hitting her in the chest and rolling off the tips of her nipples. "Some girls like men who will give them jewelry. I don't have much use for diamonds. The cows and horses aren't impressed. I like a man who isn't too proud to put in a hard day's work."

"Baby, you're an amazing, strong woman. Don't ever settle for less than you deserve."

She looked him straight in the eye and said, "I make it a point to never settle."

He pulled her into his arms and kissed her thoroughly. "I want you, more than I've ever wanted a woman before."

Pressing her breasts to his chest, she held his hand to her sex. "I want you. Now. Inside me."

"Baby, doing it in a bathtub is precarious at best. Besides, I don't have any protection. I won't do that to you."

She sighed. "Then we'll just have to finish up in here and head across the hall." For a moment, she hesitated. "Unless you really aren't that interested."

He laughed. "My interest is obvious." His hardened shaft pressed against her belly.

"Then what are we waiting for? We only have a few minutes before we have to get ready to go to the springs." She moved back and let the water rinse the soap from his body. Then she ducked beneath the spray, erasing the residual suds from her skin. When she was finished, she switched off the water, flung open the curtain and stepped out.

She didn't wait for him or offer to help.

For that, he was grateful. He had his own way of getting around, and he didn't want her feeling sorry for him.

He sat on the edge of the tub, swung his leg over and straightened, holding onto the wall as he did.

She flung a towel at him, hitting him in the chest.

He caught it in his free hand, twisted it and popped her in the ass.

She yelped. "Don't start something you can't finish," RJ warned with a sassy snarl.

He grabbed for her, swung her around until her back was against his front. Inch by inch, he dried her body, taking his time to cup her breasts, his cock nestling between her butt cheeks, teasing her with what could come next. He hoped she didn't change her mind between the bathroom and the bedroom.

"My room or yours?" he whispered into her ear.

"Mine. It's right across the hall." She turned and dried him from top to bottom, taking her time around his cock, fluffing him with the terry cloth until he thought he might explode.

"Ready?" she asked as she wrapped a towel around herself.

"More than." He reached for his prosthesis, only she beat him to it.

"you won't need that in my bed," she said.

"I need it to get across the hall."

"Hold onto me," she said. "It's only a few steps."

He hesitated.

She cocked an eyebrow. "Or are you afraid I'm not strong enough?"

"Oh, I know you're strong enough."

"Then is it because you don't want to appear weak

in front of a girl?" She shoved the prosthesis into his arms. "Whatever. We're wasting time. My father and Kujo will be back any minute. If you've changed your mind, I'll understand." She walked toward the door, swaddled in that damned towel that barely covered her ass, her long sexy legs calling to his libido. "My door will be unlocked if you care to join me."

As she reached for the doorhandle, Jake spoke, "You're right. I don't want to appear weak in front of a girl. In front of you."

"Well, I'm not suggesting you are. I only offered to save us time." She glanced over her shoulder. "What's it to be?"

He held out the fake leg without saying a word.

She came back to get it from him and wrapped a towel around his waist. "We don't want to shock the guests, should they be around."

Jake draped his arm over her shoulder. "Lead the way, woman. And I don't suppose you have a stash of protection hiding away in your room?"

Her lips quirked. "As a matter of fact, I do. A gift from well-meaning friends, encouraging me to start dating."

"I like your friends," he said as he leaned on her and hopped on his one leg toward the door.

He opened the door, and they peered out into the hallway.

"Coast is clear," he whispered.

"Then hurry," she said.

Together, they made it across the hallway into her

bedroom. No sooner had the door closed behind them, then the towels dropped and they collapsed on the bed.

RJ giggled. "I'm sure if anyone is downstairs in the great room, they heard that."

"Then we'd better give them their money's worth of entertainment." Lying in bed, Jake was on more equal terms. The missing limb wasn't as necessary to accomplish what they had set out to do.

RJ twisted around and reached into the nightstand for a box full of condoms. "Is this enough?"

He chuckled and took it from her, extracting one of the little packets. "For a month." Dropping the box back inside the drawer, he laid the packet on the nightstand.

RJ's brow puckered. "Aren't we…?"

"Not yet. I want you to be as satisfied as I will be," he said.

"Oh, I will be. Please. I want you inside me. My body aches, I want it so badly."

He chuckled. "You're going to want even more when I'm done with you."

"That's what I'm afraid of," she whispered.

He paused. "We don't have to do anything. We could just lie here and hold each other. That would be enough for me."

"Seriously?" She looked at him as if he'd grown horns. "It wouldn't be enough for me. I'll take my chances on wanting more. But rest easy. I won't expect more. You're likely to be disappointed by my performance. I'm not...how would you say? Oh, hell. I'm not experienced."

Jake frowned. "You're a virgin?"

She laughed. "Not since I was seventeen in the back of Travis Rigsby's pickup. I can't say that it was all that great."

"Usually isn't when you're a virgin." He smoothed the damp hair back from her forehead. "Since then?"

She looked past him. "I thought I was in love with a pipeliner from Wyoming doing work near Fool's Gold. We went out a couple of times, but he had a big flaw I couldn't live with."

"And that was?" Jake prompted.

"He lied." She stared up into his eyes. "He told me he was divorced. I'm ashamed to say, he wasn't. Not only was he still married, but he also had two little kids waiting for daddy to come home." Her eyes narrowed. "You're not married, are you?"

His lips curled. "A little late to be asking, don't you think?"

"No. I have a gun in my nightstand. You know I can hit what I aim at."

He held up a hand in surrender. "Yes, you can. And no, I'm not married. Never met a woman who could put up with a man who was away from home more than he was there." He held up his left hand. "You can ask Kujo to run a background check on me. I'm a confirmed bachelor. Never tied the knot."

RJ blew out a relieved sigh. "Well then, there's nothing stopping us, but time." She glanced at the clock on the nightstand. "Are you up for the challenge?"

"Are you?"

She nodded.

"Then let the game begin." He lowered himself on his arms to take her mouth in a long, slow kiss that took his breath away.

From her mouth, he moved inch by inch down her body, claiming first one breast than the other, teasing the nipples into tight buds. Continuing downward, he kissed and tongued a path over her ribs, across her belly and down to the tuft of hair covering her sex.

There, he paused and slipped his hand between thighs.

RJ parted her legs, allowing him more room to work his magic.

And he did. He wanted her to know what making love really felt like. Not making out in the backseat of a teenager's truck or being lied to by a man she thought she loved.

Jake wanted her to know how good it felt to be loved like she deserved.

CHAPTER 11

RJ's BODY burned with desire as Jake parted her folds and touched that slender nubbin of flesh packed with what felt like every nerve ending inside her.

Her back arched off the bed, and she clutched at the comforter to keep her from leaving the mattress.

"Oh, my," she gasped.

"Do you want me to stop?" he asked.

"No!" RJ couldn't breathe and didn't care if she ever drew another breath. What he was doing had to be illegal. It was better than any drug, any stimulant, anything she'd ever felt in her life.

And she wanted more.

"Please," she whispered. "Don't stop."

He touched her there again with the tip of his tongue and flicked that bundle of nerves ever so lightly.

Electrical shocks zinged from her core outward, setting her veins on fire. She raised her knees and dug her heels into the mattress, rising up to meet his talented tongue.

Jake flicked, licked and sucked on her until she teetered on the edge of eternity.

One more flick and she flew over, plunging into the first real orgasm she'd ever experienced.

He rode her with his tongue, her body quivering with each contact.

When she finally fell back to earth, she drew in a ragged breath and laughed. "So that's what it's all about." And she laughed again, joy filling her heart.

Then she reached for him, dragging him up her body. "But it doesn't feel like that's all there is."

"It's not all there is," he said, bending down to take her lips in a passionate kiss.

His mouth tasted like her sex, making RJ even more anxious to have the rest of him inside her. "Quick." She reached between them, guiding him to her entrance. "I don't think I can wait another second."

"I don't think I can either. But first..." He leaned back, grabbed the condom, tore it open and rolled it down his cock. Then he settled between her legs and kissed her again.

"We don't have to go any further," he said, his breath warm against her lips.

"The hell we don't." She grasped his buttocks and pulled him close until the tip of his erection fit into her channel.

"I'll go slow," he said. "I don't want to hurt—"

RJ pulled him into her, hard and fast, burying his shaft deep inside her.

"Well," he chuckled. "We won't go slow then."

"I said I wanted you inside me. I didn't mean in the next century," she said through gritted teeth. "It feels so right. Especially after...well after what you did."

"Mmm. You have no idea how right it feels," he said, moving in and out of her, in slow, steady motions.

Her hands still on his ass, RJ urged him to move faster and faster, until they were both breathing hard.

She dug her heels into the mattress, meeting him thrust for thrust, loving the way he filled her, stretching her channel to accommodate his girth and length.

Again, she rose to that blessed peak where everything culminated and hovered at the edge. One more thrust and she'd...

He drove deep and hard, sending her rocketing into the stratosphere, tingling sensations lighting her nerves like the Fourth of July.

Buried deep inside her, he held her close, his cock pulsing his release, his body rigid.

Together, they fell back to earth.

Jake collapsed on top of her and rolled with her to their sides. "Don't ever doubt that you're amazing. On a horse, mucking stalls and most of all, making love." He kissed her forehead, kissed her eyelids and finally kissed her lips, thrusting past her teeth to claim her tongue in a long, sensuous kiss.

When they broke apart to breathe, RJ cupped his face and smiled. "I don't know all the pretty words, so suffice it to say, wow. Just wow. You think we can do that again when we're not expected in Colorado Springs in less than an hour?"

Jake chuckled. "I was hoping you would say that." He glanced at the clock. "We'd better get going, or we'll be late."

RJ rolled out of the bed and stood, frowning. "Gunny and Kujo should have been back by now." She pulled on panties, a bra and a white button-up blouse.

Jake sat on the side of the bed and slipped into his prosthesis, applying the inner lining, the device and the outer lining.

RJ watched, unflinching. "Does it hurt?"

"It did at first. The more I wear it, the less it bothers me." He pushed to his feet and pulled her into his arms. "It allows me to be free of crutches or a wheelchair, so I can do this." He held her close and pressed a kiss to the top of her damp hair. Then he swatted her ass. "Get some pants on, or we'll be late to our meeting."

Jake wrapped a towel around his waist. "I'll be ready in less than two minutes." After checking that the hallway was empty, he left the room and entered his, closing the door behind him.

RJ pulled on her nicest pair of jeans and clean

boots, ran a brush through her hair and decided to let it hang free. It would curl around her face, but she didn't care. It made her feel more feminine. Like making love to Jake made her feel one hundred percent female. For a woman who did typically male work, she'd never felt like a normal woman. Until now.

As she straightened, the phone on the nightstand rang.

Because cell service was spotty at best in the mountains, they still had a land line. RJ answered, "Lost Valley Lodge, RJ speaking."

"RJ, it's Kujo." His words were clipped, tense.

Her stomach dropped. "What's wrong?"

"I'm in Colorado Springs at Memorial Hospital. There's been an accident."

Her heart squeezed hard in her chest. "Gunny?"

"He's been hurt, but he's stable. He didn't want me to call and worry you, but you needed to know why we hadn't made it back to the ranch."

RJ laughed, the sound ending on a sob. Gunny was her only living relative. Her father. She loved the old coot more than life. "He's going to be okay?"

"Yes. He's banged up and has a couple of broken ribs and a concussion. They're keeping him overnight for observation. He doesn't want you to come."

RJ snorted. If he was alert enough to tell her not to come, he was going to be fine. At least, she hoped he would be. "Sounds like him. Probably worried the bar won't be open on time. What happened?"

"We were on our way back from Fool's Gold after we had coffee with Marty Lange. He didn't want to meet at the ranch, said it wasn't safe. We had just left town when an SUV shot out of a side road, rammed into the side of the ranch truck and sent us spinning over the edge of an embankment."

RJ sucked in a breath. "Holy hell. There are a number of places along that road into town that are dangerous drop-offs. You two are lucky to be alive."

Kujo laughed without humor. "That's what I told Gunny. He said he was too mean to die."

A soft knock sounded on her door, and it opened to Jake. "Everything okay?" he whispered.

RJ shook her head. "Gunny's in the hospital. Someone ran them off the road on their way back from Fool's Gold."

"That Jake?" Kujo asked. "Can you put me on speaker?"

RJ hit the button on the cordless phone and Kujo's voice sounded over the speaker, "Jake?"

"Yeah, Kujo. I'm here."

"Marty Lange said Robert Henderson did make it out to his place to present an offer to purchase the Elk Horn Ranch and it's mineral rights. Emphasis on the mineral rights."

"From the mining company we're going to meet in less than an hour?"

"Yes. He told them he'd think about it. He'd been

having a tough time making ends meet. Like the Lost Valley Ranch, he relies on tourists to help fund the ranch upkeep and make payments on the equipment."

"Gunny has coffee with Marty once a month," RJ said. "Last time they met, he said he was having trouble making ends meet. Selling might have been an option for him."

"That's what Gunny said," Kujo said. "Marty wasn't ready to throw in the towel. He figured if there was an interest in the minerals, he might negotiate to lease the mineral rights. He was just checking into it when he heard Robert Henderson was murdered. He felt pretty sure Henderson was going to make the same offer to Gunny."

RJ's gaze met Jake's. "All the more reason to speak with the Omega Mining Company CEO. What do they know that we don't?"

"Does Marty think the Omega Mining Company is targeting the owners of the Lost Valley Ranch?"

"He wasn't sure, but he said someone had taken a shot at him while he'd been out riding fences. Clipped his arm. His horse threw him, and he had to walk back to the barn, but he's okay."

"Did you tell him someone took a shot at RJ?" Jake asked.

"Yes. He's worried. He thinks maybe they've discovered a vein of gold or silver running beneath the two ranches."

"How can they do that without digging to find it?"

"Apparently, Mike Orlacek found an old logbook

from the Finnian's Folly Mine, located on the Broken Wheel Ranch. It mentions a tunnel they'd been digging that stretched east to west and burrowed under the corners of the Elk Horn and the Lost Valley Ranches."

"Gold on Lost Valley Ranch?" RJ shook her head. "Is that what this is about?"

"That's what it sounds like. Marty's convinced the mining company doesn't want to wait on his answer, that they're getting rid of the ranch owners to make it easier for them to take over."

"That doesn't make sense," Jake said. "*If* the owners died, the land would be tied up in probate, much longer than if the owners sold their ranches outright. And if the deaths were suspicious, who knows how long it would take to free the land for sale?"

"We need to talk to Omega Mining," RJ said. "We're heading into the springs in a few minutes. Kujo, you were supposed to meet with us at their offices. I don't think now is the time to bail on Gunny."

"I agree. You and Jake can handle this. As it is, I got a lead on another former special forces guy named Thorn. We want to bring him into the Brotherhood Protectors. I convinced him to meet with me at the hospital."

Jake snorted. "That'll be good. Show him the job's not so cushy, huh?"

Kujo chuckled. "Something like that. He comes

with a recommendation from one of our former Army Rangers, Taz Davila."

"What's his story?" Jake asked.

"He fell during a training mission in the mountains and broke nearly every bone in his body. The incident left him with a permanent limp. With the new Army physical fitness requirements, he couldn't pass the test. A medical board booted him out."

"Another misfit, like me?"

Kujo laughed. "Aren't we all? Only we have a lot left to do before we die, don't we?"

"Damn right," Jake said.

His enthusiasm warmed RJ all the way through, and her heart swelled with something she'd never felt before.

"Anyway, he's on his way to the hospital. If he's a good fit, and he's willing, I'll hire him on the spot. That way, he can stand watch over Gunny and keep him from walking out of the hospital in nothing but a hospital gown. And I can head back to the ranch to hold down the fort until you two get back."

RJ nodded, though Kujo couldn't see her. "I'll give JoJo a call and let her know she can open the bar tonight, in case we don't get back in time."

"That'll work and make Gunny happy," Kujo said. "And if all goes according to plan, I could be back tonight as well."

RJ ended the call and shook her head. "Bastards." She looked up at Jake. "Let's get to Colorado Springs. I have a few choice words for Omega Mining."

CHAPTER 12

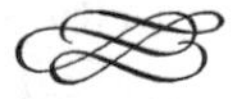

JAKE DROVE the rented SUV into Colorado Springs, RJ riding shotgun and carrying a concealed weapon beneath her jacket.

He smothered a smile. Anyone who knew RJ would be afraid if they tried hurting her or her loved ones. She'd plug a bullet in them and shoot to make a difference.

With fire in her eyes, she rode in silence most of the way through Ute pass and down the mountain into Colorado Springs.

Using the GPS on her phone, she directed him to the Omega Mining Company offices downtown in one of the few high-rise buildings. Their offices were in the penthouse at the top of the building.

When the elevator door opened, she charged out.

Jake caught her arm and steadied her. "Just remember, they don't have to tell us anything."

A frown pulled her brow into a deep V. "If they know anything, they damn well better tell us."

"They might not be responsible for the attacks on Gunny, you and Marty Lange. If you go in there loaded for bear, you might earn a personal escort out of the building with a security guard."

RJ stared into his eyes for a long moment, her chest heaving with her anger. Finally, she drew in a deep breath and let it out slowly. "Okay, I'll keep my cool." Her eyes narrowed. "But if I find out they're responsible for almost killing my father, I'll rip their hearts out of their chests and feed them to the rats."

Jake chuckled. "Remind me never to make you mad. You're kind of scary."

RJ's frown eased. "Gunny's the only family I have."

"I get that. And he's lucky he has you to look out for him."

"And vice versa," RJ said. "He'd take a bullet for me."

"Gunny's a good man."

"Yes, he is. He's always taking in strays. There are so many people who wouldn't be where they are today if not for him."

"He seems to have taken in this stray as well," Jake said. "If it hadn't been for him leasing space to the Brotherhood Protectors, we'd still be looking for a place to call home."

"And I'd be dead." RJ shook her head. "Funny how things turn out for a reason."

"Funny." He held out his hand. "Let's see what we can learn from Omega."

She held his hand until they reached the reception desk.

Jake smiled at the receptionist. "Jake Cogburn and Miss RJ Tate to see Mr. Barnes."

"Have a seat," she said. "I'll see if he's available."

Jake and RJ didn't take a seat. Instead, they walked to the windows stretching from floor to ceiling and stared out over the city of Colorado Springs. The sun shone bright over Cheyenne Mountain, and the air was clear.

"It's a beautiful day," Jake said.

"It is," RJ responded. "And it would be even better if my father wasn't in the hospital."

"Mr. Barnes will see you now," the receptionist said.

Jake turned, hooked RJ's elbow and guided her past the receptionist's desk. "Thank you." He could feel RJ tense in his grip as they stepped into the spacious office with the solid mahogany desk in the center. The window beyond gave yet another view of the city of Colorado Springs.

Frank Barnes rose from the leather seat behind the desk and rounded the corner, holding out his hand. "Miss Tate, Mr. Cogburn, I'm so glad to meet you." He looked past RJ and Jake. "I had hoped your father would accompany you, Miss Tate."

She glared at the man as he took her hand in a firm shake. "Regrettably, he couldn't make it as he's laid up in the hospital. Which you might already know."

Jake squeezed her arm.

Mr. Barnes frowned. "I'm so sorry. I didn't know he was ill."

"He's not." RJ released his hand. "Someone tried to kill him by running him off the road. Do you know anyone who would want my father dead?" RJ crossed her arms over her chest. "We know you sent a real estate broker out to make offers on my father's place and on the Elk Horn Ranch. Did you think it would be easier if, instead, the owners were dead?"

Mr. Barnes shook his head. "I'm not sure what you're getting at." He looked to Jake.

"Miss Tate might be a bit punchy as she was almost killed the same night your broker was attacked and murdered. She was then the target of a gunman, and now her father has been attacked and almost killed."

"And you think Omega Mining had anything to do with these attacks?" Frank Barnes held his hands out palms up. "What purpose would that serve? We're a legitimate mining company. I engaged Robert Henderson to represent offers for both the Elk Horn and the Lost Valley Ranches. I didn't send him out to make offers only to murder him instead. Why would I do that?"

RJ maintained her stance, though her posture loosened a bit. "I don't know. You tell me."

Jake jumped in. "Why is Omega Mining interested in the two ranches?"

"We'd really like to get the mineral rights to Finian's Folly Mine, as well as the rights on the two ranches, but Finian's Folly Mine is tied up in a conservation district. No one can mine that property. Still, we have reason to believe there's a vein of gold off a tunnel built close to the end of the mine's life that clipped the edges of the Elk Horn and Lost Valley Ranches."

Jake shot a glance toward RJ. "Like Marty Lange was saying."

"Our engineers study old mines in search of new opportunities." Barnes leaned forward. "We think there's some untapped veins we can access in that old tunnel. Our engineers are so convinced that our investors are willing to foot the bill to purchase the property and set up mining operations."

"Are they eager enough to kill to get access to the property?"

"No," Barnes said. "If they thought there was any foul play happening, they'd pull out. As of a few minutes ago, we thought Robert Henderson was the victim of an unfortunate mugging. No one mentioned other attempted murders."

RJ's eyes narrowed. "Why should I believe you, Mr. Barnes? My family has been attacked. None of this was happening before you sent your guy out to buy our property."

"We're a decent company looking to make money

and provide jobs. We're not murderers. We have one of the best safety records of any mining company in the country. We give to the communities and care about our employees. We aren't killers."

For a long moment, RJ stared into Mr. Barnes eyes.

The man spoke convincingly. Jake believed him, but he waited, letting RJ form her own opinion. After all, it was her life and Gunny's that had been threatened, not Jake's.

Finally, she dropped her arms to her sides. "I believe you, Mr. Barnes. But that doesn't solve the mystery of who would want my family and Marty Lange dead. Any clue as to who might think that would be a good idea?"

Barnes shook his head slowly. "Since they killed Mr. Henderson, I would think it's someone who's trying to stop Omega Mining from purchasing the properties. That's pure speculation on my part. Your local law enforcement folks should be chasing down the suspects."

"I don't think they know where to look."

"I have an appointment with a detective this afternoon concerning Mr. Henderson's death. At least now I know a little more about what's going on." He held out his hand to RJ. "Thank you for coming to see me. If I can provide any more information that can help you find the killer, I'd happily help. Mr. Henderson did not deserve to die. The man has a family who mourns him and grandchildren who will never know the love of their grandfather."

RJ shook the man's hand. "You know, there is something you might help us with. Do you have any maps that would indicate where the mine tunnels and shafts are that cross onto the Elk Horn and Lost Valley Ranches?"

Barnes nodded. "Actually, we do. They've been scanned from the original documents created back in the late eighteen hundreds. I can have my secretary email copies to you." He handed her a pad and paper. "Just leave your email address with me and I'll have her send them right over."

"That would be great," RJ said, scribbling an email address on the pad. "Thank you again. And I'm sorry if I came across too strong. My father means everything to me."

"I'd feel the same if it was my father," Mr. Barnes said. "I hope you and the police figure out who's behind these attacks. Until you do, we won't send any real estate brokers out to make offers on the properties."

"Thank you, Mr. Barnes," Jake said.

Jake and RJ left the CEO's office and took the elevator to the parking garage. Once in the SUV, Jake turned to RJ. "Are you okay?"

She nodded. "Is it horrible of me that I wanted Frank Barnes to be the one behind all this?"

Jake shook his head. "It would've been easier if he

was. Then at least we'd be at the root of the problem and know who to point out to the police to arrest."

"Now, we're back to square one." RJ sighed. "Do you think the state police are having any more luck than we are?"

"Let's hope they are." Jake placed his hand in the small of her back and walked her to the car. He liked touching her. She made him feel grounded and protective at the same time. He wanted to be with her, not just because she was his assignment. She was a genuinely good person.

"Next stop, Memorial Hospital," Jake said as he handed her into the passenger seat.

"You know I can open my own door, right?" she said as she climbed in and adjusted her seatbelt.

"I know," he said. "And you can probably kick my ass in a fight."

Her cheeks turned a soft shade of pink. "Thank you."

"You're welcome. And don't let any man make you feel less of a woman because he opens the door for you." He leaned in and kissed her cheek. "I open the door for you out of respect." As he turned away, he added softly, but loud enough she could hear, "and you're carrying a gun. I don't want you to shoot me."

When he climbed into the driver's seat, he glanced across at RJ.

She sat with a small smile playing on her lips. "I'm glad I met you, Jake Cogburn. You remind me that being a woman isn't something to be ashamed of."

"Good Lord, Jules, being a woman is something you should embrace and be proud of."

"Kind of like being alive?" she shot back at him.

He stiffened. Too many moments over the past months he'd wished he'd died in the explosion that had taken his leg. "Yeah."

She reached out and touched his arm. "I'm sorry. I shouldn't have said that. I can't begin to understand what you went through. All I know is that there was a reason you survived. I don't think you were done on this earth."

He nodded. "I just hope that I'm enough to keep you safe."

"So far, you've been more than enough. I wouldn't be alive today if you hadn't come along." She faced forward. "Now, if you don't mind, I don't want to get all mushy. I'm missing that female gene. It just makes me uncomfortable."

Jake laughed out loud and drove out of the parking lot, smiling.

They made it to the hospital in ten minutes and found Gunny's room.

A strange man stood outside the door, leaning against the wall.

When RJ and Jake tried to go into Gunny's room, he stepped in front of them. "Sorry, no one but the doctor and nurses can go into Mr. Tate's room."

RJ frowned. "But I'm his daughter, and this man is my bodyguard."

The man's stony expression didn't change. "Sorry,

but I was given strict instructions not to let anyone inside."

"Confound it! Let my daughter in," Gunny yelled from the other side of the door.

RJ shook her head and pushed past the man into the room. "Dad."

The man followed, placing himself between RJ and Gunny. He held up his hands. "Ma'am, you'll have to hand over your weapon before you get any closer."

"But he's my..." She shook her head. "Who the hell are you, and what are you doing in my father's room?"

"I'm Max Thornton. I've been hired to protect Mr. Tate."

Jake remembered what Kujo had said. "Thorn?"

The man nodded. "That's what they called me back in my unit."

Jake held out a hand. "Jake Cogburn. I take it Kujo hired you for the Brotherhood Protectors."

"You must be the new regional boss Kujo was talking about." Thorn gripped Jake's hand. "Good to meet you. Hell, it's good to have a job."

"I know the feeling. Kujo and Hank Patterson hired me a couple of days ago." He turned to Gunny and RJ. "We'll be based out of the Lost Valley Ranch. Gunny and RJ are the owners."

"So Kujo was telling me. Seems they're having some security issues we're helping with."

Gunny snorted. "Security, my ass. We've been attacked, and we don't know who the hell's doing it."

"If you two are finished getting to know each other, I'd like to make sure my father's alive." RJ stepped around Thorn and hurried over to the hospital bed where her father sat up with cuts and bruises on his face, a frown making him look even grumpier than usual. "Hey," she said softly.

"You shouldn't have come," he groused.

"Yeah, well, Jake made me," she said.

"Someone needs to be there to open the bar and get food on the table for the guests."

"I left a roast in the crockpot for supper. All I need to do is make a salad, and dinner will be ready. JoJo is all set to open the bar. And I'm guessing Kujo is on his way to help."

Her father's frown deepened. "So, you've got things handled. I don't need to be here. I feel fine." He drew in a deep breath and winced. "Except when I breathe deeply."

"Then don't breathe deeply, Dad." She smiled down at him. "They only want to keep you one night. It won't kill you."

"Maybe not, but who'll keep what happened to me from happening to you?"

"That's what Jake is doing," she said.

"We didn't see it coming. That guy shot out of nowhere." Gunny reached out to grasp her hand. "I don't know what I'd do without you, Jules. I need to be home where I can keep an eye on you."

"I feel the same, Dad. But you need to be where the medical staff can keep an eye on you. Concussions are serious business. If you get bleeding on the brain, you need to be where they can help you. Out at the ranch, you'd just die."

"But I feel fine."

"Humor me, Dad. Stay the night. Everything will run fine for one night without you. I'll make sure of it."

"And I'll be there to protect her," Jake said.

Thorn stepped forward. "And I'll be here to protect you, Mr. Tate."

"Call me Gunny," RJ's father said. "Mr. Tate was my father."

"Yes, sir," Thorn said.

"Dad, we have to go, if we want to get supper on the table and take care of the bar." RJ leaned over her father and kissed his cheek. "I love you."

He reached out and patted her hand. "Promise me you'll be safe."

"I promise," RJ said. "Get some rest."

"That's all I can do here," he muttered.

Jake and RJ left the hospital and headed back through Ute Pass to Fool's Gold and out to the Lost Valley Ranch. All the way, Jake was extra vigilant, slowing at blind curves and watching out of the corner of his eye for vehicles darting out of nowhere.

Kujo had been with Gunny, and he hadn't been enough to keep the older man from being injured.

Jake prayed he'd be enough to protect RJ.

. . .

RJ ALMOST WANTED to refund all of their guests money and send them home. She was afraid they might become collateral damage if whoever was trying to kill her and Gunny clipped one of the guests in their crossfire.

Once at the ranch, she checked in on Kujo and JoJo. They had the Watering Hole up and running and the patrons taken care of there.

Jake and RJ headed for the lodge to get supper on the table for the guests there.

When she entered the kitchen, she was greeted with the savory aroma of roast beef. The scent reminded her that she hadn't had lunch. Her belly rumbled in response. She didn't have time to eat. Not yet. Their guests would expect a meal in the next thirty minutes.

Once again, Jake proved helpful in the kitchen. Between the two of them, they cut up a salad, ladled roast beef onto plates and carried the plates out to the guests in the dining room. Once they'd all been served, Jake and RJ sat down to eat a quick dinner. Then they made plates of food for JoJo and Kujo and carried them across to the Watering Hole.

RJ and Jake took over while Kujo and JoJo ate their dinner. The crowd of patrons was slightly smaller than usual but was just as thirsty. RJ mixed drinks while Jake waited tables, keeping a close eye on RJ.

By the time Kujo and JoJo took over, RJ found herself exhausted.

"Go get some sleep," JoJo insisted. "Kujo and I can finish up here and close the bar."

"I'm going to take you up on that. I can barely keep my eyes open," RJ yawned.

"Go," JoJo said. "We've got this."

RJ left the bar with Jake. Striker followed her back to the lodge and found his bed in the great room.

RJ locked the doors and headed up to her room, her pulse quickening with every step she climbed.

Jake was right behind her.

Would he follow her all the way to her bedroom? Would they make love into the wee hours of the morning and wake tired but satisfied?

She had her hand on her doorknob when she turned to see Jake had his hand on his.

She'd initiated their first time in bed together by inviting him into her shower. If he wanted to be with her, he'd have to initiate it this time.

RJ entered her room and left her door unlocked. For a long moment, she waited, watching the doorknob, hoping it would turn and Jake would come in.

When he didn't, her disappointment weighed heavily on her.

Was once enough for him?

Well, it wasn't for RJ. She wanted so much more from Jake.

Apparently, he didn't feel the same.

RJ stripped out of her nice clothes, pulled on an

oversized T-shirt and climbed into her bed. The drawer on the nightstand was slightly open. She started to push it closed but saw the box of condoms inside and opened it instead.

Maybe he was giving her the option to rest without being bothered.

She grabbed a packet from the box, swung her legs over the side of her bed and padded to her door. With her hand on the doorknob, she leaned close, listening.

Nothing.

Son of a bitch. Steeling her nerves, she yanked open her door and ran smack into Jake standing on the other side, his fist raised to knock.

RJ blinked up at him. "Oh, it's you."

He smiled. "Expecting someone else?"

She shook her head, grabbed the front of his shirt and dragged him across the threshold into her room.

Her heart rejoiced.

He'd come to her.

RJ handed him the condom packet. "Care to put this to good use?"

He smiled and took the packet from her fingers. "I thought you'd never ask."

They stripped. Jake removed his prosthesis, and the next hour was magical with Jake bringing her to the edge and beyond, and then making love to her.

Afterward, they lay naked in each other's arms and fell asleep.

RJ snuggled close and didn't wake until she heard

the sound of Striker pawing at the door, whining. When his whining didn't produce the desired movement, he barked. And the barking became more insistent.

"What the hell?" RJ muttered as she rose to her feet, pulled on her T-shirt and a pair of sweatpants. The dog probably needed to go outside. She opened the door.

Expecting Striker to rush in, she was surprised when he grabbed the hem of her shirt and tried to drag her out of her room.

"Hey," she said. "I'm not dressed to go outside. I need shoes." Then she smelled it.

Smoke.

CHAPTER 13

JAKE GRABBED HIS PROSTHESIS, cursing it's clumsiness and wishing he could run out the door instead of stopping to put on his leg.

RJ disappeared with Striker. Footsteps sounded in the hallway, and banging sounded on doors as RJ shouted, "Everyone, get out of the lodge!"

A smoke alarm screamed to life as people rushed down the stairs.

By the time Jake had on his leg and pants, he was the last person in the hallway. He ducked his head into each room, calling out, "Everyone out?"

When he was certain there weren't any stragglers left behind, he descended the stairs.

Kujo met him at the bottom, his T-shirt pulled up over his mouth and nose. "Everyone is out on the front lawn." The man coughed and blinked his eyes.

"Go," Jake said. "Stay with RJ. If someone set this

fire, he might stick around to make sure she dies in it."

"You should go be with her."

"I'm not the one with a baby on the way and wife waiting for me to come home," Jake said. "Just do it."

Kujo nodded and left the lodge.

The smoke was heaviest coming from the kitchen. He grabbed a tablecloth from one of the dining tables, wrapped it around his face and felt the swinging door to kitchen. It wasn't too hot, so he pushed inward and choked on the smoke, billowing from around the edges of the door leading into the basement.

Grabbing the fire extinguisher from the wall near the stove, he felt the door to the basement. It wasn't super-hot, which led him to believe the fire hadn't heated to a flashpoint.

He opened the door, hit the light switch and waited for the smoke to clear a little. Thankfully, the light was still working, but it didn't help much bouncing off the smoke.

Tucking the tablecloth closer around his face, he rushed down the stairs.

His eyes stung, and his nostrils and lungs burned, but he plowed forward, feeling his way. He pulled at his memory, trying to recall where he was headed based on his visit to the basement with Kujo and Gunny when they were discussing its conversion into a base for the Brotherhood Protectors Colorado division.

A cool breeze wafted toward him, pushing the fog into his face. Ahead, he spied a bright red and orange wall of flame where a stack of empty wooden crates had been.

Jake aimed the fire extinguisher at the flame's base and let loose a stream of the carbon dioxide mixture. He didn't waiver, attacking the fire relentlessly until the retardant completely smothered the flames and nothing was left but smoke and ash.

He gave the source of the flames a thorough dousing, emptying the fire extinguisher.

As the smoke settled, that cool breeze led him toward a broken basement window. Someone had thrown something through it. Probably a Molotov cocktail.

When he was certain the flames wouldn't resurge, he climbed the stairs and exited the kitchen through the back door. It was possible the person responsible was still on the grounds, lingering to view his handiwork.

Though the night air was cold on Jake's naked chest, he breathed in the clean air, trying not to cough and alert the culprit.

Moving into the shadows, Jake searched the tree line, hoping to find the bastard who'd tried to burn down the lodge with people in it. When his search came up empty, he circled around the side to the front where guests stood in the yard, huddled in their night clothes with blankets wrapped around them.

RJ stood at the front door, calling into the smoke-filled interior, "Jake! Damn it, Jake! Get your ass out here. The lodge can burn to the ground for all I care as long as you're not in it."

Kujo stood behind her, using his body as a shield should someone decide to shoot at the rancher's daughter.

Striker tugged at her shirt, urging her to back away from the lodge and the black haze issuing from inside. Thankfully, the smoke was lessening, and soon, would stop altogether.

"Jake!" she yelled, her voice catching on a sob.

"I'm here," he called out, hurrying to her side.

She turned and flung herself into his arms. "Damn you," she murmured, her lips pressed to his smokey skin. "I thought the smoke got to you."

Kujo laid a hand on his back. "Dude, we were about to go in after you."

"I'm okay," he said and coughed, his throat scratchy and irritated. But he was alive.

"We used the phone in the bar to call 911," Kujo said. "The fire department should be on its way out now.

The distant sound of sirens confirmed Kujo's prediction.

Soon, the yard was filled with fire trucks, an ambulance and two sheriff's vehicles.

Sheriff Richard Barron stepped out of his vehicle. Deputy Gathright and the fire chief joined him as they met Kujo, Jake and RJ on the front porch.

Jake explained what he'd found in the basement

and how he'd extinguished the fire. The emergency medical technicians checked Jake over and suggested he go to a hospital to make sure he didn't have any lasting effects from smoke inhalation.

"I'm okay," he said and returned to RJ's side. His throat felt like hell, but he was glad to be out in the open air, not in a hospital emergency room.

The firefighters entered the building. After a few minutes, the fire chief came out to report, "The fire's out, thanks to Mr. Cogburn. However, as he suspected, it appears to be a case of arson. We'll have to conduct an investigation. In the meantime, we recommend your guests stay somewhere else tonight."

RJ nodded. "I'll arrange to put them up at the Iron Mountain Lodge. Can they go inside to collect their belongings?"

The fire chief nodded. "Yes, but after we've aired some of the smoke out of the lodge. One of my guys will have to escort them one room at a time."

After the firefighters opened all the windows in the lodge and the air cleared, RJ organized the guests. One couple at a time, they entered the building, collected their belongings and carried them out.

Jake walked with RJ to the bar to place a call to the Iron Mountain Lodge, securing three rooms for the displaced guests. RJ grabbed a roll of trash bags from the storage room before they headed back to the lodge.

She handed out the trash bags to the guests. "Put

your things in this before you place them in your vehicles. That way you don't make your cars smell like smoke. Lost Valley Ranch will pay to have your clothes and suitcases cleaned to get the smell out. Does anyone need a driver to get you to the Iron Mountain Lodge?"

Mrs. Pendergast raised her hand. "My husband and I have difficulty driving at night. If we could follow someone, that would help."

"I can lead you all out there," Deputy Gathright offered. "When you're ready. No hurry."

Soon, a caravan of the three guests' vehicles and the deputy's SUV left Lost Valley Ranch.

Once the guests were gone, RJ found the fire chief. "What about us?" She motioned to herself, Kujo and Jake. "Can we stay in the lodge? Is it safe?"

The chief frowned. "As long as you stay out of the basement where the fire began, it'll be all right."

The fire chief and firefighters packed up their equipment and rolled out of the yard.

Sheriff Barron stood staring at the lodge. "I remember the day your father bought this place. He was so proud to be a landowner."

"And he still is," RJ said. "Though, sometimes, I wonder if it would've been easier or he'd have been better off, if he'd taken a job as a greeter at a big box store. I'm sure it would've been a lot less stress and heartache in his life."

"Your father is a man who needs to work hard. He'd have been miserable." The sheriff hugged RJ.

"Sheriff," Kujo stepped forward, "if the new security system is working like it should, we might be able to get some video of whoever set that fire. Jake and I will look through the feed tonight."

The sheriff pulled a card out of his wallet and handed it to Kujo. "That has my cellphone number on it. Let me know what you find. I don't care if it's day or night. I'll move on it. If we have a clear image, we can use it as evidence to get a conviction."

"Will do," Kujo said. "Thanks for getting everyone out here so fast."

"We take fire seriously around here," the sheriff said. "Even a small unattended campfire can end up burning thousands of acres and homes."

Jake nodded. "I know. As dry as it's been, the forests are tinderboxes waiting for a match to set them off." Every year fires tore through the state, destroying old forests and many homes.

"Exactly." Sheriff Barron frowned. "Do I need to leave a deputy out here to keep an eye on the place?"

Kujo shook his head. "We'll be all right tonight. I'm sure none of us will sleep. And tomorrow Gunny will be back. We'll try to do some cleaning in the areas that won't impact the fire chief's investigation."

After the sheriff left, Kujo, Jake and RJ entered the lodge.

The stench of smoke made them cough.

"Hopefully, the smoke didn't damage the computers in the study." Kujo headed for Gunny's office. The door had been closed throughout the fire.

The fire fighters had opened the windows inside and closed the door again, keeping the majority of the smell and lingering smoke from entering.

Kujo booted the computer and waited.

Jake stood with RJ at the window, staring out at the night.

"Gunny's going to be devastated," she said softly.

Jake slipped an arm around her. "He's a tough old bird. He'll be all right."

"I know. It's just hard to see your dreams go up in smoke." She laughed, though the sound held no humor. "Literally, up in smoke."

"Insurance should cover the cleanup," Jake said. "And the time without guests will give us all a chance to stop whoever is determined to drive you out before anyone else is hurt."

"And we'll have time and space to complete the renovations," Kujo added from his seat behind Gunny's desk. "One month, and we'll be up and running again, all shiny and clean."

RJ smiled. "You make it sound so easy."

"It is, when you hire the right people," Kujo said. "With Thorn coming on board and more recommendations to look into, Jake will have his work cut out for him." Kujo held up a hand. "Don't worry, I'm not leaving him to fend for himself until the current issue is resolved."

"Good to know you've got my six," Jake said.

"Ah." Kujo looked up from the computer. "I'm on,

and the security cameras did their magic. Come help me review."

Jake and RJ rounded the desk and stood looking over Kujo's shoulder at the monitor, watching the video footage from the camera that overlooked the side of the house where the basement window had been broken.

Starting at a point after midnight, they reviewed footage. For the first hour they sped through the feed. Nothing moved at the rear of the building, not even a barn cat or rabbit. They were able to speed through most of it, going through two hours of video in under thirty minutes.

Jake blinked, his eyes sore and tired from lack of sleep and being bombarded with smoke. He rubbed his hands across his face and almost missed the shadowy figure that emerged at the edge of the monitor and quickly disappear.

"Wait," Jake said. "Back it up."

Kujo reversed the video slowly.

"There." Jake pointed to the screen.

Kujo stopped the reverse and played the video forward slowly.

A man wearing a Denver Broncos ballcap ran past the camera, tossed something at the side of the building and kept going.

"Back it up again and zoom in," Jake said.

Kujo reversed the video and adjusted the zoom.

RJ pointed. "He's looking up…right…there." She

jabbed her finger at the screen and frowned. "I know him."

"You know him?"

"Yes. That's Larry Sarley. He comes to the Watering Hole sometimes. The man's a mean drunk. Once, we had to call the sheriff out when he picked a fight with one of our other customers." She glanced up, her lips forming a tight line. "Call the sheriff. We need to bring that bastard in."

Kujo dialed the sheriff and reported what they'd found. He compressed a copy of that portion of the video and sent it to the sheriff's email address, grumbling as he did. "Swede's our computer guru. He'd have this all sewn up in seconds."

Jake grunted. "I'd like to meet Swede and reconnect with Hank, someday."

"I'm sure they'll be down to help get this place set up once the wiring guys do their thing," Kujo said. When he was done, he sat back and glanced at Jake and RJ seated together on a small couch in a corner of the study. "It's going to be daylight soon. Why don't you two catch some shut-eye?"

Jake tightened his arm around RJ's shoulders. "We could, you know. I don't think there was that much smoke in the bedrooms."

RJ reached out to pat Striker's head where he lay next to them on the couch. "Too much to do." She yawned and closed her eyes for a moment. "I wish this was all over. What if they can't find Sarley? What if he gets away?"

"Other than you calling the sheriff on him, why would he want to hurt you and Gunny?" Jake asked.

"I don't know." RJ rolled her head back on Jake's shoulder. "That incident was months ago. If he was going to get his revenge, why didn't he do it then?"

"It can't be just what you and Gunny did to him," Kujo pointed out. "Why would he have targeted and killed Robert Henderson, if he was indeed the one who did that?"

"And why attack Marty?" Jake shook his head. "Is there more than one person involved in these attacks? And is there more than one motivation?"

"We might know more when they apprehend Sarley and bring him in for questioning." Kujo pushed to his feet and glanced down at RJ. "In the meantime, what do you want to accomplish before Gunny's released from the hospital?"

"I'd like to scrub the kitchen of all the smoke we can remove and start the laundry with everything we can wash that way. Although, it won't do any good to clean sheets until we get the smell out of the walls, furniture and rugs." She looked around the room. "It's overwhelming at this point."

"Why don't we start by feeding the animals in the barn?" Jake said. "The sun's just starting to come up. Everything will look better in the sunshine."

"It's supposed to be cloudy today," RJ contradicted.

"Cloudy or sunshine, the horses won't care as long as they're getting fed." Jake extended his hand

and pulled her to her feet. "We owe Striker a steak for waking us." He bent and scratched the dog behind the ears. "Just proves you don't need four good legs to be a hero."

Striker jumped down from the couch and leaned his body against Jake's leg.

"I think he'd like a steak," RJ said. "Since we won't have guests for a while, I'm sure we could spare a steak for our hero." She straightened and stretched her arms toward the ceiling. "Let me change into my jeans and boots, and I'll be ready to start the day."

"I'll meet you on the porch when you're ready," Jake said.

RJ and Striker left the study, heading to the second level and her room.

Kujo stared across the office at Jake. "I get the feeling this isn't just about revenge on the Tates."

"I got the same feeling," Jake said. "It has to have something to do with the mine. Someone didn't want Robert Henderson to secure a land purchase for the Omega Mining Company. And after our meeting with the mining company's CEO, I don't think it was them."

"Then who?" Kujo asked.

"Could Larry Sarley be working for someone else? Someone who knew Larry was primed to vent his anger on the Tates?"

Kujo picked up the phone on Gunny's desk. "We have to call Hank and fill him in. He'll probably have Swede do a background check on Larry Sarley. When you get a chance, ask RJ if she knows who Larry works for?"

Jake nodded. "Will do." He left Kujo talking to Hank and hurried up to his room, where he pulled on a T-shirt and a light jacket. The morning mountain air had a bite to it.

He'd just stepped out of his room when RJ came out of hers with Striker.

She'd pulled on a pair of jeans, her boots, a blue chambray shirt and a denim jacket. Jake would also bet she had her handgun tucked into the shoulder holster beneath the jacket. Her hair was secured at the nape of her neck in a ponytail, making her look young and innocent.

With no makeup and her hair pulled back from her face, she was still the most beautiful woman Jake had ever known. Her beauty was more than her outer appearance. She was gorgeous all the way through.

Jake opened his arms.

RJ stepped into them. "I think I died a thousand deaths when you didn't come out of the house right away."

He chuckled. "Sounds like you're getting used to having me around."

"I am," she admitted.

"And you might even like me a little." He brushed a loose strand of her hair back behind her ear.

"Don't get ahead of yourself," she said, her brow wrinkling. "But yeah, I guess I do like you."

"Good, because I kind of like you, too." He tipped

her chin upward and stared down into her eyes. "Is there room in your heart for a broken-down SEAL?"

She shook her head. "No."

His heart sank to his knees.

RJ cupped her hand against his cheek and leaned up to press a kiss to his lips. "There's room in my heart for a strong man whose life has great meaning and who is here today with so much more to give." She leaned back and frowned at him. "You realize you're my hero."

His chest tightened, and warmth spread throughout his body. "I don't know about that."

"Well, you are." She stepped back. "Come on, I know some horses who couldn't care less about our conversation. They just want to be fed."

Jake chuckled and followed RJ out of the house, Striker trotting alongside them.

They were halfway to the barn when a thunderous boom echoed off the ridges.

Jake grabbed RJ and pushed her to the ground, throwing his body over hers.

Striker dropped to his belly and inched closer to RJ.

For a moment, Jake remained frozen, his mind and body reliving the explosion that took his leg.

Then he remembered where he was and that RJ was his responsibility to keep alive.

RJ was right. There was a reason he hadn't died that day. That reason was to make sure RJ didn't die today.

CHAPTER 14

"THAT WAS CLOSE," RJ said. "Too close. Like I think it was on Lost Valley Ranch." She wiggled beneath Jake.

He rolled to the side, lurched to his feet and held out his hand to RJ. "How close?"

"By the sound, it could be around the Stephensville ghost town." She met his gaze. "Or the mine just above there. It takes some nerve to blast into a mine on private property." Her jaw tightened. "Come on. We're going to check it out."

"Let me tell Kujo where we're going. We might need backup."

"You do that. I'll saddle horses."

"Wouldn't it be faster to take the ATVs?" he asked.

"Yes, but noisier. We can get closer without being detected on horseback."

"Right." Jake spun. "Stay inside the barn until I get back."

"Okay." RJ entered the barn, her gun drawn, and

closed the door behind her. After ascertaining the barn was empty but for her and the horses, she holstered her gun and brought out Reggie and Doc.

By the time Jake entered the barn, she had the saddles on both horses and was in the process of slipping a bridle over Doc's nose.

"Kujo got word that Gunny and Thorn are on their way home from the hospital. Gunny's doctors couldn't hold him down a moment longer. I told Kujo where we were headed. He said he'd join us as soon as Gunny and Thorn get here."

"Good. Gunny will know where we're headed and can lead them up here."

"Kujo brought up a good point after you left."

"Yeah?" She handed Reggie's bridle to Jake.

He took it and fit it on his horse's nose. "Larry Sarley could be working for someone else. He has reason enough to want revenge on the Tate's, but not necessarily Marty Lange, and no reason to kill Robert Henderson. If he's responsible for all of this, what would he get out of it?"

RJ shrugged. "It's not like he owns land or has the funds to buy property. He can barely keep a job. He was fired from the feed store for being lazy. The casino let him go for stealing. The last I heard, he was working as a ranch hand."

"For whom?" Jake asked.

RJ closed her eyes tightly. A moment later, they opened wide. "The Broken Wheel Ranch."

Jake swore. "Isn't that the one with Finian's Folly Mine?"

She nodded. "Mike Orlacek owns that property."

"And it's tied up in a conservation district, which means he can't mine on his land."

RJ frowned. "We know Mike. He's been a friend since we bought Lost Valley Ranch."

"Has he ever expressed an interest in purchasing Lost Valley?"

Her frown deepened. "Seems like maybe he has. But that's been a while. At least a year ago."

"Wouldn't hurt to have the sheriff question him after he apprehends Sarley." Jake checked the tightness of the girth and led the horse out of the barn.

RJ was right behind him, Striker on her heels. "Mike doesn't have the funds to set up a mining operation. Why would he stop the sale to a company that does?"

"We won't know until we question Orlacek." Jake paused outside the barn. "If you wait a minute, I'll let Kujo know to check into the owner of the Broken Wheel Ranch."

RJ shook her head. "If someone is up there blowing up the shaft on Lost Valley Ranch, I want to catch them in the act."

"It would be better to have backup," Jake said.

"The longer we wait, the more chance they have of getting away."

"Promise me you won't go in guns-ablazin'," he said. "We're going to look, not make a citizen's arrest." He pulled his cellphone from his pocket. "We can snap pictures to use as evidence."

"Fine. I promise not to go in shooting. Now, can we get up there before they get away?"

With a frown, Jake nodded. "It's against my better judgement, but I'm sure you'd go without me if I insist we stay here."

"I'll get the gate," RJ said and led her horse out of the barn.

Jake stuck his fake foot in the stirrup and swung up in the saddle, amazed at how natural it was getting. He rode Reggie through the gate and waited for RJ to close and latch it.

She mounted and took off across the pasture.

Jake rode alongside her until they entered the trail between the trees and had to proceed single-file. Striker raced ahead. The dog got along just fine with three good legs. Though he was missing his back foot, it didn't slow him down.

RJ hoped that Jake would take a page out of Striker's book and learn that he was every bit as good a man as any, even with one missing leg. Hell, he was a better man than many.

When they reached the tiny ghost town, RJ didn't slow. She kept going, climbing up the hillside that led to the abandoned shaft that had been boarded up since she could remember.

As they neared the top of the hill, she slowed her mount and raised her fist to silently bring Jake to a halt behind her.

She dismounted and tied her horse to a tree.

Just over the top of the ridge was a level area and the entrance to the mine shaft. She couldn't see it from where she was standing, but then if someone was up there, they wouldn't see her or Jake.

On foot, they climbed the rest of the way, pausing just short of the top to peek over the edge.

RJ swore softly beneath her breath. "The boards and the metal grate have been moved. Someone's been in that shaft."

Jake looked to where the boards had been thrown to the side and a big metal grate had been tossed on top of them.

Striker leaped over the top of the hill.

"Striker, heel," RJ called out.

Too late.

Striker ran out into the open and into the mine shaft.

"No. No. No." RJ started over the top of the hill.

Jake grabbed her arm and held her back. "You can't go in there after him," he whispered. "Even if the people with the dynamite have cleared out, the shaft isn't stable."

"I know that. Striker will be killed if I leave him in there. Some shafts have vertical drops of hundreds of feet. If he slips into one of those, he could die from the fall. I won't leave him to die." She shook loose of Jake's hand and ran after Striker.

. . .

JAKE HAD no choice but to go after the woman and the dog. He pulled his handgun from beneath his jacket and half-ran, limping toward the shaft entrance over the rocky terrain.

Once inside, he used the flashlight on his cellphone to light his way over rocks, old iron rail tracks and debris.

RJ wasn't far ahead, having reached the limit of the light coming into the tunnel from outside.

"Let me go first," he said.

"No," RJ said. "Striker only comes to me."

"Stubborn woman. Then hold this." Jake handed her the cellphone.

RJ took the phone and shined the beam in front of her. "Striker," she called out softly.

Dust still stirred in the shaft, though most had already settled.

Jake stayed close to RJ, ready to pull her back if they came across a vertical shaft, and ready to knock her aside if someone loomed in front of her holding a weapon. He didn't like that she was in the lead. Entering the shaft was insane, but he couldn't let her go in alone.

Twenty yards into the shaft, the tunnel split in two directions in a Y.

"Which way did he go?" RJ worried.

"Listen. Maybe you'll hear him." Jake stood perfectly still.

RJ cocked her head and listened.

A faint tapping sound came from the tunnel on

the left, like that of a dog's toenails clicking against rock.

RJ hurried to the left, holding the light high enough she could see ahead.

Jake stumbled along behind her, trying not to trip over the rocks that had fallen from the ceiling, possibly in the last explosion. The roof of the tunnel wasn't reinforced with beams to keep the weight of the mountain from crashing down on top of them.

A chill slithered down his spine as they moved deeper into the mine.

Ahead, the sound of a dog's whine echoed against the walls.

"Striker," RJ said and moved faster.

Jake struggled to keep up with her, tripping over rocks and the old rails.

Soon, the light bounced off an obstruction in the tunnel.

RJ came to a halt. "Striker?"

Jake caught up with her about the time she spotted the dog.

Striker sat near the obstruction, looking toward RJ.

"Striker, come," she said.

The dog remained where he was. Sitting. Looking toward her as if proud of an accomplishment.

Then it hit Jake. "Where did you get Striker?"

"I adopted him from the Air Force Academy kennels."

"He's a Military Working Dog?"

"He was. Until he lost his back foot in an explosion."

"What did he do for the military?"

"He was a bomb-sniffing...dog." RJ's eyes rounded. "Shit."

Jake nodded. "Shit is right. Get behind me. I'm going to grab Striker, then we're going to get the hell out of here."

"He's not used to you. He might bite."

"It's a chance we have to take." He moved RJ behind him and inched toward Striker, looking for the explosive materials he'd sniffed out.

When he was within grabbing distance, he reached out to the dog with his fist. "Good boy. Heel."

Striker looked from Jake to RJ and remained seated.

Jake murmured, "He probably expects to be rewarded with his toy."

"I don't have it. It's back at the lodge." RJ's voice shook, causing the light to dance. "Let me grab him by the collar."

"No. Stay where you are. If all hell breaks loose, get out. Don't wait for me or Striker. Just get out."

"I'm not going anywhere without you and Striker."

"Why did I expect you to say that?" He shook his head and bent to scoop his hands under the animal.

Striker growled low in his chest but didn't snap at Jake.

Jake straightened, holding the sixty-pound dog

against his chest. He turned and started toward RJ. "Go."

She turned and shined the light forward, moving quickly and steadily, shining the light backward whenever an obstruction got in Jake's way.

Not that he could see over the dog in his arms. He did the best he could, feeling his way with his good foot and stumbling when his prosthesis encountered an impediment.

Striker didn't fight his hold, and for that, Jake was grateful.

A loud bang sounded further down the tunnel, like the report of gunfire.

Striker jerked in Jake's arms.

"Wait," Jake said.

"There's only one way out," RJ said. "The way we came in." She pulled her gun out and held it in front of her. "We have no choice."

"Then hold onto Striker while I go ahead." He set the dog on the ground, holding tightly to his collar.

RJ took over control of the animal.

Jake didn't let go of the dog until RJ had a firm grip on him.

He took the light from her and led the way.

When they arrived at the Y in the tunnel, he stopped. "Son of a bitch."

RJ came up beside him with Striker.

The entrance to the shaft had been covered with the metal grate that had been lying on top of the wooden boards.

A heavy ore bucket stood in front of the grate, holding it in place.

A lump on the rails in front of the grate stirred and groaned. It was a man.

All Jake could see was the man's silhouette.

"He shot me," the man said. "That bastard shot me." His voice was weak and accompanied by a gurgling rasp.

RJ started to go to the man.

Jake held her back. "Don't."

A voice shouted from outside the mine entrance, "Thanks for making this easy."

"You bastard, you shot me," the man on the ground said, his voice fading. "I did everything you asked me to."

"And you tried to blackmail me," the outside guy said.

"Mr. Orlacek?" RJ called out.

"Yeah. Like it matters that you know who's been mucking around in your mine. In a few minutes, you'll all be buried beneath a ton of rocks. No one will know."

"Why, Mr. Orlacek?" RJ beseeched. "I thought you, Marty and Gunny were friends."

"They would've sold out to that fancy schmancy mining company. Some rich bastard would've gotten all that gold that should've come to me from Finian's Folly Mine. I inherited that mine. That gold belongs to me."

"Killing Marty and Gunny wouldn't get you that gold. Why did you try?"

"It would've kept Omega from coming in and setting up a huge mine. I've been working the Folly a little at a time. I've been putting back gold for a decent retirement. I just needed a little more time. Omega wouldn't have given that to me. So, I'm shutting it down, blowing the tunnels. If I can't have that gold, no one will have it. Not Omega, not Marty and not Gunny."

"Mr. Orlacek, you don't have to do this. Gunny doesn't want that gold, and he doesn't want to sell Lost Valley. He just wants to run his ranch and bar and be happy doing it."

"Yeah? Well, when you inherit it from Gunny, you'll sell it. That damned conservation district my grandfather allowed to be assigned to the land tied my hands. I can't mine what belongs to me. And those tunnels from my mine onto your property still belong to me. I should get the gold from them. Not Omega or any other bigshot mining conglomeration. The mining stops here. It's over."

"Get back down the other tunnel," Jake said. "Now." He grabbed her arm and dragged her into the right tunnel away from the one Striker had found the explosives in. "Run," he said. Holding onto her hand, he dragged her and Striker deeper into the mountain, praying that this tunnel led far enough away from the other that the explosion wouldn't affect it.

They'd gone another hundred steps into the

opposite tunnel when a loud boom shook the mountain.

"Get down!" Jake yelled. He threw her to the ground and covered her body with his.

Rocks broke from overhead and crashed down on him, pummeling his back with the force. Dust filled the tunnel, choking off the little bit of light his cellphone produced.

"Cover your mouth and nose," he cried out, pulling his T-shirt up to do the same. He closed his eyes and willed the ground to quit shaking and the ceiling to hold.

When the earth stilled, Jake moved. Rocks and gravel rolled off his back. He pushed to his knees and felt for RJ beneath him. "Jules, sweetheart. Are you all right?"

For a moment, she said nothing. Then she shifted beneath him. "I'm all right," she said and coughed. "Striker?"

The dog whined and came to stand in front of her. He licked her face and whined again.

"Good boy," she said and laughed. "We're alive."

Jake pushed to a sitting position and shined the cellphone light around the tunnel.

Behind them, the tunnel had collapsed with rocks piled high, blocking their escape. In the other direction, the tunnel was relatively intact. Where it went, he didn't have a clue.

"I figure we only have an hour or less left on the battery in my cellphone, if that much," he said.

"We aren't getting out that way," RJ said, looking back. "Are we trapped?"

"I saw a copy of the map Barnes sent. These shafts have vents that lead to the surface. It was the way they kept fresh air coming in for the miners to breathe. We can wait here and hope someone finds us and digs us out without collapsing the tunnel further, or we can follow this tunnel and see if it leads to one of the air vents."

"I'm not one to sit around and wait to die. Let's find our own way out of here." RJ stood, brushed the dust off her and followed Jake through the tunnel.

Jake prayed it didn't lead to a dead end. The explosion could've made different parts of the mine collapse. He hoped this tunnel had been spared, and that it led out of the mountain.

"Just so you know, I like you more than a lot," Jake said as they walked along. "I have to believe that we lived through that explosion for a reason. If it's for no other purpose than for you to take me to a Sadie Hawkins dance, I'm good with that."

RJ laughed. "I believe we're still alive so we can get out of here and turn Orlacek over to the authorities for the murders of Larry Sarley and Robert Henderson. And we can't let him hurt Gunny."

"That, too." He reached for her hand and held it as they walked through the tunnel. "But I'm really looking forward to dancing with you again."

"And you will. I haven't given up hope."

If RJ could be positive, so could Jake. He'd dig

with his fingers to get them out of there. Damn it, they couldn't die. Not now. Not when they'd just found each other.

Striker ran ahead of them.

"Think he's found some more dynamite?" RJ asked.

"God, I hope not," Jake said.

The farther they went, the wetter the floor of the tunnel became until they were slogging through an ankle-deep stream.

Jake's pulse kicked up. "Do you see light ahead?" Jake fumbled with the cellphone. "I'm turning off the cellphone flashlight. Don't worry. I can turn it back on."

He turned off the light and held his breath while his vision adjusted.

Ahead, he could see a faint glow.

"It is a light," RJ said, her voice excited.

Striker barked from a long way away.

Jake turned the flashlight back on. "Come on. Striker's onto something."

Still holding hands, they started to run, stumbled and nearly fell and then slowed to a fast walk, picking their way over the rubble beneath the surface of the stream flowing at their feet.

The tunnel made a gentle curve to the right. Ahead, the glow was a bright light shining in from a small opening where the stream flowed through it.

Striker stood on a ledge near the opening, as if waiting for them.

When they approached, he jumped into the water and swam to the opening and disappeared.

"Striker!" RJ cried out.

When he didn't return, she squeezed Jake's hand. "If nothing else, he made it out."

"If he can make it out, so can we. I'll go first and check it out."

Handing RJ the cellphone, Jake waded toward the small hole. The frigid water got deeper, until it was up to his waist. His teeth chattered, and he fought to keep from being swept through with the current. He didn't know what was on the other side. For all he knew it could be a two-hundred-foot drop.

One step at a time, he moved forward. The gap between the water and the top of the tunnel was only a couple inches. He'd have to go under to get out. "I'll see you on the other side," he said and ducked beneath the surface. The current lifted him and forced him through the opening.

CHAPTER 15

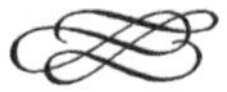

As the man she was falling in love with disappeared beneath the water, RJ took several steps forward. "Jake!"

She waded deeper, the chill of the stream taking her breath away. "Jake!"

Her heart froze in her chest, and she couldn't remember how to breathe. "Oh, sweet Jesus, please."

"Jules," Jake's voice echoed from the other side.

RJ let go of the breath she'd been holding in a whoosh. She stumbled forward, still holding the cellphone lighting her way. Before she reached the opening to the tunnel, the current whipped her feet out from under her.

She barely had time to suck in air when she plunged beneath the surface. Moments later, she was out of the tunnel, falling a short distance to a pool of icy cold water.

She only went under for a moment when strong

arms surrounded her and pulled her to the surface. The water was only four feet deep when she got her feet beneath her.

"Come on. We need to get out of this before we freeze." Jake held her hand as they waded to the shore.

Striker stood on the bank of a stream, shaking water from his thick coat.

Once out of the water, RJ wrapped her arms around Jake's neck. "That scared me," she admitted.

"It was just a little swim."

"No. It scared me that you disappeared. I didn't know if you were alive or dead." She hugged him again and leaned up on her toes to kiss him hard on the mouth.

He laughed and held her close. "We're not out of the woods yet. Orlacek is still on the loose, and your father should be back at the lodge, if not on his way to find us."

"Damn. I didn't t-think about that. We h-have to get back to the mine entrance before Gunny does. Orlacek is bat-shit crazy and dangerous."

"Based on the direction the tunnel led from the shaft entrance, we can follow this mountain around this side, and we should come out just below where we entered."

Shivering, RJ started the hike around the side of the mountain, climbing over rocks and through crevices. If it was tough going for her, she could imagine how hard it was for Jake.

Still, he kept up, never complaining.

RJ saw the horses in the distance, down below the ridge. They were almost back around.

At that moment, the sound of small engines caught her attention. She glanced down the hill at three approaching four-wheelers.

"No," she cried. "We're not going to get there before they do."

"We will," Jake said. "And if we don't, we'll be there in time to save them. I promise."

They ran faster, slipping on the rocks, picking themselves up and continuing forward. Every step brought them closer to helping her father, Kujo and Thorn.

Still too far away to yell over the sound of the engines, RJ watched as the ATVs shot over the top of the ridge.

Moments later, they heard the sound of gunfire.

Striker cowered low, and then shot away from them, heading up the hill.

"Striker, no!" RJ ran faster. When she reached the top of the hill, she burst out into the open, with her gun drawn, praying it would work after being submerged in the icy stream.

Gunny, Kujo and Thorn were hunkered low behind giant boulders while Michael Orlacek waved his handgun, using the ore bucket for cover. "It's too late. No one will get that gold now. No one."

"Mike, I don't care about the gold. I just want my daughter," Gunny called out.

"She's dead. Buried in that mine shaft. You heard the explosion. She's inside, trapped, dead, I tell you."

"You're wrong," RJ called out. "You blew up the wrong tunnel."

Orlacek turned his gun toward her.

RJ raised hers and pulled the trigger. Nothing happened.

A shot was fired.

RJ looked down at her body, waiting for the bullet to hit and pain to rip through her. When it didn't, she glanced up.

Michael Orlacek swayed, his eyes wide, his gun dangling from his fingertips. Then he crashed to the ground and lay still.

RJ turned to find Jake breathing hard, the hand holding his gun slowly lowering to his side.

"Woman," he ground out hoarsely, "don't ever scare me like that again."

She ran to him and wrapped her arms around his waist. Then she turned to the men coming out from behind the boulders.

"Anyone hurt?" Jake asked.

"My pride and a few scrapes and bruises," Gunny grumbled, holding his bleeding arm. "I didn't think we'd be shot at coming over the top of the rise. Need to check the four-wheelers. We had to ditch them in a hurry."

"We were just about to take him out when RJ came out of nowhere. She was between us and the gunman," Kujo said.

"That's Mike Orlacek," Gunny said, gazing down at the body. "That crazy son of a bitch. I should've known he was behind this. He tried to give me a low-ball offer for the Lost Valley Ranch a year ago. When I refused, he got all belligerent. Haven't spoken to him since."

"He had Larry Sarley kill Robert Henderson," RJ said. "Then he killed Larry and buried him in the mine shaft." She tipped her head toward the rubble that had been the entrance into the tunnel.

"He said he buried you alive in there," Gunny closed the distance between himself and his daughter, taking her into his arms for one of those bear hugs she'd always loved. "I'm glad he didn't succeed. I don't know what I'd do without you."

"I'm useless; I couldn't shoot that bastard."

"That's why you have Jake around." Gunny shot a glance toward Jake. "Thank you."

Jake nodded. "I'm just glad we got here in time."

"Guess we'll be spending lots of time together in the future," Gunny held out his hand, "if you still want to make Lost Valley Ranch home to the Brotherhood Protectors in Colorado."

"I'm still in, if your daughter wants me to hang around."

She hooked her arm through his elbow and leaned into him. "He promised to go with me to the Sadie Hawkins Dance. He might change his mind after he sees how hopeless I am dancing the two-step."

"The hell you are." Gunny puffed out his chest. "I taught you everything I know. It's the reason why her mother—"

"—fell in love with you," RJ smiled into her father's eyes. "Nothing says love like a man who can dance, right?"

"Damn right." Gunny grinned and shot a narrow-eyed glance at Jake. "Remember that."

Jake gave him a serious look. "Yes, sir."

RJ hooked her father's arm and walked toward one of the ATVs. "Let's get back to the lodge and get the sheriff up here."

"This one's got a bullet through the engine," Kujo said from one of the ATVs. "It won't start."

"You got a way back?" Gunny asked.

RJ nodded. "Our horses are tied up just below the ridge."

"Kujo, you can ride with me," Gunny said.

"No," Kujo said. "Someone should stay with the body. I can do that."

Gunny and Thorn climbed onto the ATVs, while Jake and RJ walked back down the hill to where the horses waited.

Minutes later, they were back at the lodge.

Sheriff Barron arrived with an ambulance and a recovery team to get Orlacek down from the hills. It would take longer to get to Sarley's body.

RJ didn't really care if they left Orlacek for the buzzards and Sarley entombed in the mine. They'd gotten what they'd deserved.

The big question on her mind and in her heart was where did she and Jake go from here? Yeah, he owed her a date to the Sadie Hawkins dance, but what about between now and Friday? What about afterward?

She spent the afternoon cleaning the walls in the kitchen and every pot, pan, plate, glass and utensil. They'd have to work on one room at a time to get all the smoke off the walls and furniture.

The insurance company promised to send out a smoke mitigation company before the end of the week to help with the rest of the lodge and to gut the basement of the fire damage.

After a supper of grilled cheese sandwiches and tomato soup, RJ and Jake cleaned the dishes and put them away.

"I'm going for a shower and bed," she announced to the men seated at the dining table, who'd been discussing what had happened that day. RJ was tired and strangely depressed and anxious.

Never had she been as unsettled as she was at that exact moment.

She climbed the stairs and looked back. Even Striker was content to hang out in the dining room with the guys.

Fine. She didn't have the corner on the Jake market. He wasn't hers to claim, and Striker had the run of the house.

She grabbed the clothes she'd run through the washer and dryer and entered the bathroom. She turned the lock, thought about it and unlocked it. If he wanted to join her in the shower…

RJ stripped, switched on the shower and stepped behind the curtain, her breath catching and holding, her hearing attuned to the sound of a door opening.

She finally had to breathe and wash her hair and body. The water got cold, forcing her to end her shower, and still, he hadn't come to join her.

Had everything they'd gone through scared him away from her? Had being trapped in the tunnel been all one-sided in bringing her closer to him, but not him closer to her?

Why couldn't she let go of her worry instead of stewing on it well after the water heater ran out of hot water?

She dressed and walked across the empty hallway. Alone. Suddenly, going to bed seemed so… so…depressing.

For a long moment, she stood with her hand on her doorknob, not wanting to go into her cold, empty room.

This was ridiculous. She had to sleep sometime. Squaring her shoulders, she pushed the door open and entered.

"I thought you'd never get here," a voice said from her bed.

Jake lay on the coverlet, fully clothed in a clean T-shirt and sweatpants, his hair slicked back and damp. He had his hands laced behind the back of his neck, and he smiled.

"You can tell me to leave if you don't want me here. I'll understand," he said.

"I thought you'd had enough of being with me," RJ said.

"That's as far from the truth as you can get." He sat up and patted the bed beside him.

"I left the door to the bathroom unlocked," she mumbled.

He nodded. "I know."

"You knew, but you didn't come in."

"I remembered how challenging it was the last time and wanted to get a shower before I came to you."

She settled on the bed beside him. "Why do I feel awkward and shy all of a sudden?"

He laughed. "I felt the same. Without the threat of someone trying to kill you, I feel like we're starting all over."

"Exactly." She sat with her hands in her lap. "Can we just move past this stage and get to the good stuff? I'm too old to play games and pretend I don't like you when I do. So very much." She turned to him. "And I want to get naked with you and make love until the sun comes up. Why does this have to be so hard?"

He gathered her in his arms and held her. "It doesn't have to be hard. Not when we feel the same way about each other."

Her heart lifted. "You do? You feel like that?"

"What was the word you used the first night?" he laughed. "Confused?"

She shook her head. "That was the first night. I'm not confused anymore. I know what I want."

"You do?" he asked, capturing her face between his hands. "What do you want, Jules?"

She sighed. "I want you."

He brushed his thumb across her lips. "That's a good thing because I want you, too. Confused or convinced, I want you. You're an amazing, brave woman with a heart of gold. I don't need riches to be happy. I need you."

RJ's heart swelled in her chest making her feel as if she could explode with the enormity of her emotions. "Well, cowboy, what are we waiting for? Isn't it time we get to the good stuff?" She reached for the hem of her T-shirt, tore it over her head and tossed it to the floor.

"Being with you is the good stuff. The rest is just icing on the cake."

EPILOGUE

"I CAN'T BELIEVE you actually wore that dress." JoJo grinned and looked at her friend from top to toe. "It looks amazing…and risqué."

"I feel like every part of my body is exposed." RJ tugged at the fabric around her bosom. The corset pushed everything up, making her breasts look two sizes larger than normal.

JoJo turned RJ around and gave her a little shove out into the street of the Fool's Gold ghost town. Hundreds of people waited to see Madame LaBelle gun down the dastardly gang leader to free the miners from terror. "Hurry out there and perform your shoot out. I'm ready to get to the Sadie Hawkins Dance and kick up my heels."

"Did you find a date?" RJ asked.

JoJo shook her head. "No. And I don't need one. I get along just fine without a man in my life."

"Well, as your friend, I thought you might try to avoid the commitment of asking someone to go the Sadie Hawkins Dance with you. So, I found you a date."

"What?" JoJo squeaked. "You shouldn't have."

"Too late." RJ grinned.

"No really. You shouldn't have." JoJo's heart beat faster and her hands grew clammy.

RJ laughed and leaned close. "He's right behind you."

JoJo spun and had to back up a couple of steps to get a good look at the tall, broad-shouldered man. "Oh, my," she whispered.

"JoJo, this is Max Thornton.," RJ turned to JoJo. "Thorn, this is my good friend Josephina Angelica Barrera-Rodriguez."

JoJo stared into the iciest blue eyes she'd ever fallen into. "JoJo."

He chuckled as he took her hand and held it a little longer than a normal handshake. "Excuse me?"

JoJo's cheeks heated. "Sorry. My friends call me JoJo."

"JoJo." He smiled. "My friends call me Thorn."

"Nice to meet you." JoJo held onto Thorn's hand a little longer than necessary. She liked how warm and strong it was and had that strange feeling that she didn't want to let go. It was a new feeling since her stint in the Army. One she wasn't sure she could trust. She hadn't known many men she felt truly safe around since she left active duty. Gunny was one of them. He was good to the core. Any others…well, she wasn't taking any chances.

"How long have you known RJ?" JoJo asked, shooting a glare toward her friend. Now that she'd gotten her into this "date", how was she supposed to get out of it?

"I've known RJ all of three days. We met that day Michael Orlacek tried to bury her in a mine shaft."

"Oh." She blinked up at him, her heart hammering against her ribs. It was worse than she'd thought. RJ didn't know this man. He was a complete stranger. She didn't know what he might be capable of or if he was a good man or a bad man. Looks could be deceiving. Actions were what counted.

JoJo pushed her shoulders back and stood as tall as her five feet two inches could make her. "Look, you don't have to go to the Sadie Hawkins Dance. RJ shouldn't have asked you to take me. It's tradition for the woman to ask the man. Since I didn't ask you, you're not obligated to escort me."

She let that sink in, hoping he'd be happy to take the proffered exit and bow out gracefully.

He shook his head. "I'd be more than happy to take you. I'm going either way. At least with a date, I won't have to stand around by myself." He grinned. "I hate being the wallflower." His smile faded. "My only caution is that I'm not that graceful on the dance floor." He tapped his right leg. "I'm recovering from an accident."

JoJo studied the man.

He walked a few steps away and back with a noticeable limp. "See? It's kind of hard to keep in step."

So, the man had a limp. That meant he probably couldn't run fast. If he tried anything with her, all she had to do is run faster than him. That shouldn't be a problem. She was in shape, ran on a daily basis and could easily outrun a man with a limp. This date might work out.

"Okay. But I came in my own car. I'll go home in my own car. Alone."

His lips quirked. "Yes, ma'am. It's only a dance. Nothing else. Gotcha."

JoJo stood beside Thorn as RJ rocked the role of Madame LaBelle and pretended to shoot the gang leader who'd terrorized the mining camp of Fool's Gold, freeing them from fear.

If only it were that easy, JoJo would have killed the person who'd attacked her, raped her and left her for dead. Only thing was, she didn't know who he was. That particular memory had been locked inside her head for the past year since she'd left the military.

She lived in her own fear of running into the man again and not knowing it was him.

For all she knew, it could be Max Thornton.

A shiver rippled down her spine.

Thorn appeared to be a nice man. JoJo couldn't live her entire life in fear of every man she met. She'd come in her own car and would leave in her own car. She'd trained in Krav Maga self-defense and could take down a man twice her size. What could go wrong?

When the shootout was over and Madame LaBelle claimed Jake as her date for the dance.

Thorn turned to JoJo and held out his hand. “Shall we?”

She stared at him for a long time, trying to read his every thought and coming up with a blank. JoJo placed her hand in Thorn’s and prayed she wasn’t making a big mistake. But then, they were going to a dance, not going to a dark alley between huts in the desert of Afghanistan where she could be forced to the ground, raped and strangled until she passed out.

“Hey.” Thorn squeezed her hand gently. “I promise not to step on your toes or hurt you.”

JoJo looked up into those beautiful blue eyes. “I’m counting on you to keep me safe,” she whispered.

“I will,” he said. “I promise.”

JoJo wished her therapist and friend, Emily was already at the dance. She’d know what to do to keep JoJo from having a full-on panic attack. Emily knew her story and the fallout JoJo had been dealing with since. RJ meant well by finding JoJo a date, but she didn’t know. Didn’t understand.

JoJo walked into the dancehall, wondering if she could hold herself together as easily as Thorn held her hand.

ROCKY MOUNTAIN RESCUE

COMING SOON

New York Times & USA Today
Bestselling Author

Rocky Mountain Rescue

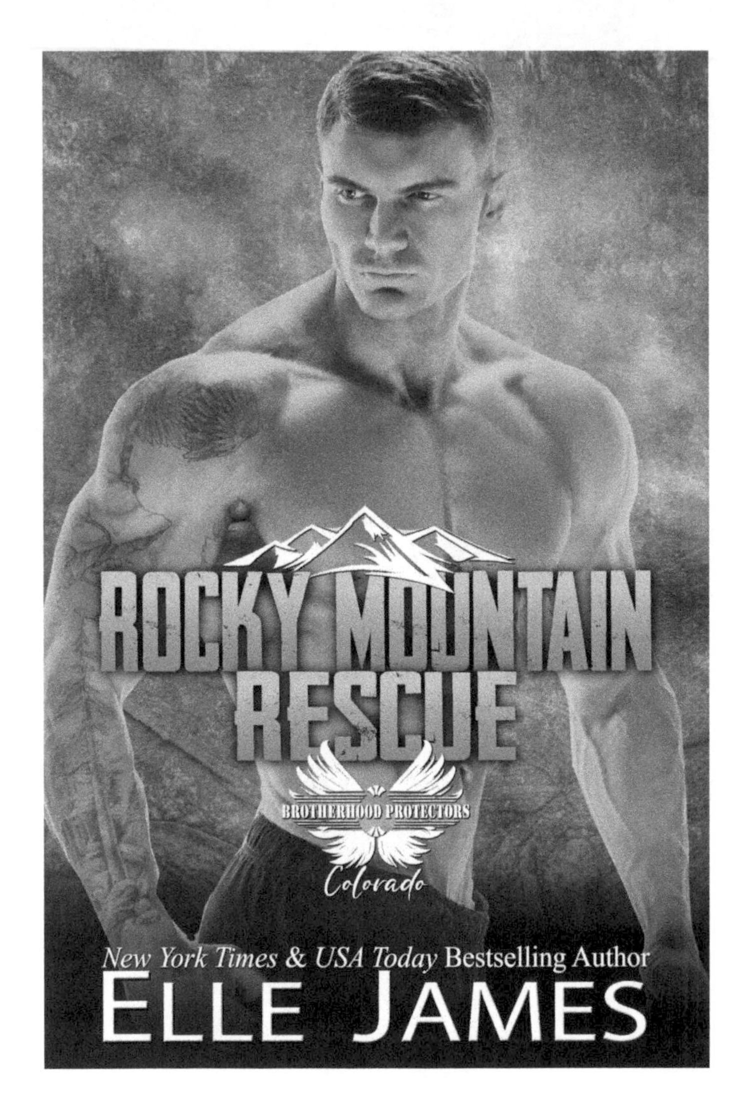
ROCKY MOUNTAIN RESCUE
BROTHERHOOD PROTECTORS
Colorado
New York Times & USA Today Bestselling Author
ELLE JAMES

ABOUT ROCKY MOUNTAIN RESCUE

BROTHERHOOD PROTECTORS COLORADO
BOOK #2

FORMER GREEN BERET MAX THORNTON'S career ended when he fell two hundred and fifty feet during a training exercise and broke nearly every bone in his body. Left with a permanent limp and in need of a job, he is recruited by Brotherhood Protectors where he can use his combat training and skills to protect, guard and rescue others. He didn't expect his first assignment to be the resident mechanic bar waitress. Nor did he expect the mechanic to be a spitfire of a female with a whole lot of anger.

JOSEPHINA ANGELICA BARRERA-RAMIREZ OR JOJO, as her friends call her, prefers to be left alone with the work she does on the machinery and vehicles of the Lost Valley Ranch. Suffering from situational amnesia brought on by an attack she sustained during a deployment to Afghanistan, she's touchy about being touched and doesn't take any flack from ranch guests or the Brotherhood Protectors operating out of the lodge. When she becomes the target of a shadowy figure in the night, a former Green Beret is assigned as her bodyguard until the attacker can be found and neutralized. Forced to have the Green Beret around, her distrust of men is challenged and the wall around her heart crumbles.

When danger threatens all they come to mean to each other, Max and JoJo must fight their own fears to defeat evil while losing the battle of their hearts to win a future together.

Rocky Mountain Rescue

BREAKING SILENCE

DELTA FORCE STRONG BOOK #1

New York Times & *USA Today*
Bestselling Author

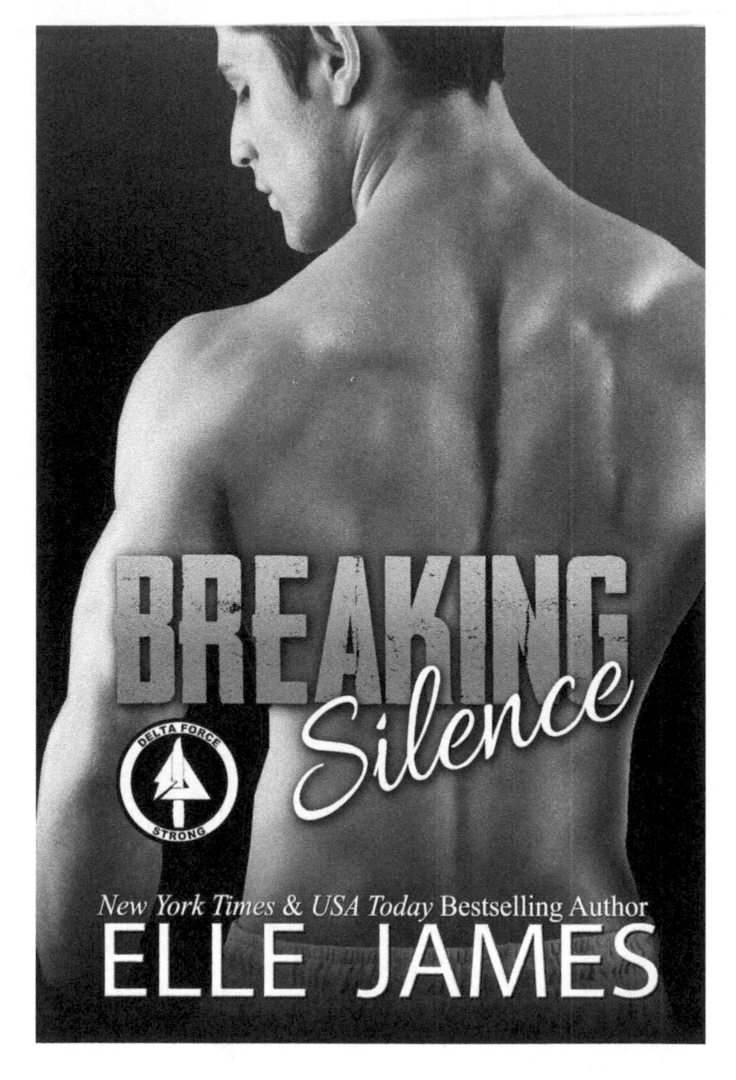
BREAKING
Silence
DELTA FORCE
STRONG
New York Times & USA Today Bestselling Author
ELLE JAMES

CHAPTER 1

HAD he known they would be deployed so soon after their last short mission to El Salvador, Rucker Sloan wouldn't have bought that dirt bike from his friend Duff. Now, it would sit there for months before he actually got to take it out to the track.

The team had been given forty-eight hours to pack their shit, take care of business and get onto the C130 that would transport them to Afghanistan.

Now, boots on the ground, duffel bags stowed in their assigned quarters behind the wire, they were ready to take on any mission the powers that be saw fit to assign.

What he wanted most that morning, after being awake for the past thirty-six hours, was a cup of strong, black coffee.

The rest of his team had hit the sack as soon as they got in. Rucker had already met with their commanding officer, gotten a brief introduction to the regional issues and had been told to get some rest. They'd be operational within the next forty-eight hours.

Too wound up to sleep, Rucker followed a stream of people he hoped were heading for the chow hall. He should be able to get coffee there.

On the way, he passed a sand volleyball court where two teams played against each other. One of the teams had four players, the other only three. The four-person squad slammed a ball to the ground on the other side of the net. The only female player ran after it as it rolled toward Rucker.

He stopped the ball with his foot and picked it up.

The woman was tall, slender, blond-haired and blue-eyed. She wore an Army PT uniform of shorts and an Army T-shirt with her hair secured back from her face in a ponytail seated on the crown of her head.

Without makeup, and sporting a sheen of perspiration, she was sexy as hell, and the men on both teams knew it.

They groaned when Rucker handed her the ball. He'd robbed them of watching the female soldier bending over to retrieve the runaway.

She took the ball and frowned. "Do you play?"

"I have," he answered.

"We could use a fourth." She lifted her chin in challenge.

Tired from being awake for the past thirty-six hours, Rucker opened his mouth to say *hell no*. But he made the mistake of looking into her sky-blue eyes and instead said, "I'm in."

What the hell was he thinking?

Well, hadn't he been wound up from too many hours sitting in transit? What he needed was a little physical activity to relax his mind and muscles. At least, that's what he told himself in the split-second it took to step into the sandbox and serve up a heaping helping of whoop-ass.

He served six times before the team playing opposite finally returned one. In between each serve, his side gave him high-fives, all members except one—the blonde with the blue eyes he stood behind, admiring the length of her legs beneath her black Army PT shorts.

Twenty minutes later, Rucker's team won the match. The teams broke up and scattered to get showers or breakfast in the chow hall.

"Can I buy you a cup of coffee?" the pretty blonde asked.

"Only if you tell me your name." He twisted his lips into a wry grin. "I'd like to know who delivered those wicked spikes."

She held out her hand. "Nora Michaels," she said.

He gripped her hand in his, pleased to feel firm pressure. Women might be the weaker sex, but he didn't like a dead fish handshake from males or females. Firm and confident was what he preferred. Like her ass in those shorts.

She cocked an eyebrow. "And you are?"

He'd been so intent thinking about her legs and ass, he'd forgotten to introduce himself. "Rucker Sloan. Just got in less than an hour ago."

"Then you could probably use a tour guide to the nearest coffee."

He nodded. "Running on fumes here. Good coffee will help."

"I don't know about good, but it's coffee and it's fresh." She released his hand and fell in step beside him, heading in the direction of some of the others from their volleyball game.

"As long as it's strong and black, I'll be happy."

She laughed. "And awake for the next twenty-four hours."

"Spoken from experience?" he asked, casting a glance in her direction.

She nodded. "I work nights in the medical facility. It can be really boring and hard to stay awake when we don't have any patients to look after." She held up her hands. "Not that I want any of our boys injured and in need of our care."

"But it does get boring," he guessed.

"It makes for a long deployment." She held out her hand. "Nice to meet you, Rucker. Is Rucker a call sign or your real name?"

He grinned. "Real name. That was the only thing my father gave me before he cut out and left my mother and me to make it on our own."

"Your mother raised you, and you still joined the

Army?" She raised an eyebrow. "Most mothers don't want their boys to go off to war."

"It was that or join a gang and end up dead in a gutter," he said. "She couldn't afford to send me to college. I was headed down the gang path when she gave me the ultimatum. Join and get the GI-Bill, or she would cut me off and I'd be out in the streets. To her, it was the only way to get me out of L.A. and to have the potential to go to college someday."

She smiled "And you stayed in the military."

He nodded. "I found a brotherhood that was better than any gang membership in LA. For now, I take college classes online. It was my mother's dream for me to graduate college. She never went, and she wanted so much more for me than the streets of L.A.. When my gig is up with the Army, if I haven't finished my degree, I'll go to college fulltime."

"And major in what?" Nora asked.

"Business management. I'm going to own my own security service. I want to put my combat skills to use helping people who need dedicated and specialized protection."

Nora nodded. "Sounds like a good plan."

"I know the protection side of things. I need to learn the business side and business law. Life will be different on the civilian side."

"True."

"How about you? What made you sign up?" he asked.

She shrugged. "I wanted to put my nursing degree

to good use and help our men and women in uniform. This is my first assignment after training."

"Drinking from the firehose?" Rucker stopped in front of the door to the mess hall.

She nodded. "Yes. But it's the best baptism under fire medical personnel can get. I'll be a better nurse for it when I return to the States."

"How much longer do you have to go?" he asked, hoping that she'd say she'd be there as long as he was. In his case, he never knew how long their deployments would last. One week, one month, six months...

She gave him a lopsided smile. "I ship out in a week."

"That's too bad." He opened the door for her. "I just got here. That doesn't give us much time to get to know each other."

"That's just as well." Nora stepped through the door. "I don't want to be accused of fraternizing. I'm too close to going back to spoil my record."

Rucker chuckled. "Playing volleyball and sharing a table while drinking coffee won't get you written up. I like the way you play. I'm curious to know where you learned to spike like that."

"I guess that's reasonable. Coffee first." She led him into the chow hall.

The smells of food and coffee made Rucker's mouth water.

He grabbed a tray and loaded his plate with eggs, toast and pancakes drenched in syrup. Last, he stopped at the coffee urn and filled his cup with freshly brewed black coffee.

When he looked around, he found Nora seated at one of the tables, holding a mug in her hands, a small plate with cottage cheese and peaches on it.

He strode over to her. "Mind if I join you?"

"As long as you don't hit on me," she said with cocked eyebrows.

"You say that as if you've been hit on before."

She nodded and sipped her steaming brew. "I lost count how many times in the first week I was here."

"Shows they have good taste in women and, unfortunately, limited manners."

"And you're better?" she asked, a smile twitching the corners of her lips.

"I'm not hitting on you. You can tell me to leave, and I'll be out of this chair so fast, you won't have time to enunciate the V."

She stared straight into his eyes, canted her head to one side and said, "Leave."

In the middle of cutting into one of his pancakes, Rucker dropped his knife and fork on the tray, shot out of his chair and left with his tray, sloshing coffee as he moved. He hoped she was just testing him. If she wasn't…oh, well. He was used to eating meals alone. If she was, she'd have to come to him.

He took a seat at the next table, his back to her, and resumed cutting into his pancake.

Nora didn't utter a word behind him.

Oh, well. He popped a bite of syrupy sweet

pancake in his mouth and chewed thoughtfully. She was only there for another week. Man, she had a nice ass…and those legs… He sighed and bent over his plate to stab his fork into a sausage link.

"This chair taken?" a soft, female voice sounded in front of him.

He looked up to see the pretty blond nurse standing there with her tray in her hands, a crooked smile on her face.

He lifted his chin in silent acknowledgement.

She laid her tray on the table and settled onto the chair. "I didn't think you'd do it."

"Fair enough. You don't know me," he said.

"I know that you joined the Army to get out of street life. That your mother raised you after your father skipped out, that you're working toward a business degree and that your name is Rucker." She sipped her coffee.

He nodded, secretly pleased she'd remembered all that. Maybe there was hope for getting to know the pretty nurse before she redeployed to the States. And who knew? They might run into each other on the other side of the pond.

Still, he couldn't show too much interest, or he'd be no better than the other guys who'd hit on her. "Since you're redeploying back to the States in a week, and I'm due to go out on a mission, probably within the next twenty-four to forty-eight hours, I don't know if it's worth our time to get to know each other any more than we already have."

She nodded. “I guess that’s why I want to sit with you. You’re not a danger to my perfect record of no fraternizing. I don’t have to worry that you’ll fall in love with me in such a short amount of time.” She winked.

He chuckled. “As I’m sure half of this base has fallen in love with you since you’ve been here.”

She shrugged. “I don’t know if it’s love, but it’s damned annoying.”

“How so?”

She rolled her eyes toward the ceiling. “I get flowers left on my door every day.”

“And that’s annoying? I’m sure it’s not easy coming up with flowers out here in the desert.” He set down his fork and took up his coffee mug. “I think it’s sweet.” He held back a smile. Well, almost.

“They’re hand-drawn on notepad paper and left on the door of my quarters and on the door to the shower tent.” She shook her head. “It’s kind of creepy and stalkerish.”

Rucker nodded. “I see your point. The guys should at least have tried their hands at origami flowers, since the real things are scarce around here.”

Nora smiled. “I’m not worried about the pictures, but the line for sick call is ridiculous.”

“How so?”

“So many of the guys come up with the lamest excuses to come in and hit on me. I asked to work the nightshift to avoid sick call altogether.”

"You have a fan group." He smiled. "Has the adoration gone to your head?"

She snorted softly. "No."

"You didn't get this kind of reaction back in the States?"

"I haven't been on active duty for long. I only decided to join the Army after my mother passed away. I was her fulltime nurse for a couple years as she went through stage four breast cancer. We thought she might make it." Her shoulders sagged. "But she didn't."

"I'm sorry to hear that. My mother meant a lot to me, as well. I sent money home every month after I enlisted and kept sending it up until the day she died suddenly of an aneurysm."

"I'm so sorry about your mother's passing," Nora said, shaking her head. "Wow. As an enlisted man, how did you make enough to send some home?"

"I ate in the chow hall and lived on post. I didn't party or spend money on civilian clothes or booze. Mom needed it. I gave it to her."

"You were a good son to her," Nora said.

His chest tightened. "She died of an aneurysm a couple of weeks before she was due to move to Texas where I'd purchased a house for her."

"Wow. And, let me guess, you blame yourself for not getting her to Texas sooner…?" Her gaze captured his.

Her words hit home, and he winced. "Yeah. I should've done it sooner."

"Can't bring people back with regrets." Nora stared into her coffee cup. "I learned that. The only thing I could do was move forward and get on with living. I wanted to get away from Milwaukee and the home I'd shared with my mother. Not knowing where else to go, I wandered past a realtor's office and stepped into a recruiter's office. I had my nursing degree, they wanted and needed nurses on active duty. I signed up, they put me through some officer training and here I am." She held her arms out.

"Playing volleyball in Afghanistan, working on your tan during the day and helping soldiers at night." Rucker gave her a brief smile. "I, for one, appreciate what you're doing for our guys and gals."

"I do the best I can," she said softly. "I just wish I could do more. I'd rather stay here than redeploy back to the States, but they're afraid if they keep us here too long, we'll burn out or get PTSD."

"One week, huh?"

She nodded. "One week."

"In my field, one week to redeploy back to the States is a dangerous time. Anything can happen and usually does."

"Yeah, but you guys are on the frontlines, if not behind enemy lines. I'm back here. What could happen?"

Rucker flinched. "Oh, sweetheart, you didn't just say that..." He glanced around, hoping no one heard her tempt fate with those dreaded words *What could happen?*

Nora grinned. "You're not superstitious, are you?"

"In what we do, we can't afford not to be," he said, tossing salt over his shoulder.

"I'll be fine," she said in a reassuring, nurse's voice.

"Stop," he said, holding up his hand. "You're only digging the hole deeper." He tossed more salt over his other shoulder.

Nora laughed.

"Don't laugh." He handed her the saltshaker. "Do it."

"I'm not tossing salt over my shoulder. Someone has to clean the mess hall."

Rucker leaned close and shook salt over her shoulder. "I don't know if it counts if someone else throws salt over your shoulder, but I figure you now need every bit of luck you can get."

"You're a fighter but afraid of a little bad luck." Nora shook her head. "Those two things don't seem to go together."

"You'd be surprised how easily my guys are freaked by the littlest things."

"And you," she reminded him.

"You asking *what could happen?* isn't a little thing. That's in-your-face tempting fate." Rucker was laying it on thick to keep her grinning, but deep down, he believed what he was saying. And it didn't make a difference the amount of education he had or the statistics that predicted outcomes. His gut told him she'd just tempted fate with her statement. Maybe he was overthinking things. Now, he was worried she wouldn't make it back to the States alive.

* * *

NORA LIKED RUCKER. He was the first guy who'd walked away without an argument since she'd arrived at the base in Afghanistan. He'd meant what he'd said and proved it. His dark brown hair and deep green eyes, coupled with broad shoulders and a narrow waist, made him even more attractive. Not all the men were in as good a shape as Rucker. And he seemed to have a very determined attitude.

She hadn't known what to expect when she'd deployed. Being the center of attention of almost every single male on the base hadn't been one of her expectations. She'd only ever considered herself average in the looks department. But when the men outnumbered women by more than ten to one, she guessed average appearance moved up in the ranks.

"Where did you learn to play volleyball?" Rucker asked, changing the subject of her leaving and her flippant comment about what could happen in one week.

"I was on the volleyball team in high school. It got me a scholarship to a small university in my home state of Minnesota, where I got my Bachelor of Science degree in Nursing."

"It takes someone special to be a nurse," he stated. "Is that what you always wanted to be?"

She shook her head. "I wanted to be a firefighter when I was in high school."

"What made you change your mind?"

She stared down at the coffee growing cold in her mug. "My mother was diagnosed with cancer when I was a senior in high school. I wanted to help but felt like I didn't know enough to be of assistance." She looked up. "She made it through chemo and radiation treatments and still came to all of my volleyball games. I thought she was in the clear."

"She wasn't?" Rucker asked, his tone low and gentle.

"She didn't tell me any different. When I got the scholarship, I told her I wanted to stay close to home to be with her. She insisted I go and play volleyball for the university. I was pretty good and played for the first two years I was there. I quit the team in my third year to start the nursing program. I didn't know there was anything wrong back home. I called every week to talk to Mom. She never let on that she was sick." She forced a smile. "But you don't want my sob story. You probably want to know what's going on around here."

He set his mug on the table. "If we were alone in a coffee bar back in the States, I'd reach across the table and take your hand."

"Oh, please. Don't do that." She looked around the mess hall, half expecting someone might have overheard Rucker's comment. "You're enlisted. I'm an officer. That would get us into a whole lot of trouble."

"Yeah, but we're also two human beings. I wouldn't be human if I didn't feel empathy for you and want to provide comfort."

She set her coffee cup on the table and laid her hands in her lap. "I'll be satisfied with the thought. Thank you."

"Doesn't seem like enough. When did you find out your mother was sick?"

She swallowed the sadness that welled in her throat every time she remembered coming home to find out her mother had been keeping her illness from her. "It wasn't until I went home for Christmas in my senior year that I realized she'd been lying to me for a while." She laughed in lieu of sobbing. "I don't care who they are, old people don't always tell the truth."

"How long had she been keeping her sickness from you?"

"She'd known the cancer had returned halfway through my junior year. I hadn't gone home that summer because I'd been working hard to get my coursework and clinical hours in the nursing program. When I went home at Christmas..." Nora gulped. "She wasn't the same person. She'd lost so much weight and looked twenty years older."

"Did you stay home that last semester?" Rucker asked.

"Mom insisted I go back to school and finish what

I'd started. Like your mother, she hadn't gone to college. She wanted her only child to graduate. She was afraid that if I stayed home to take care of her, I wouldn't finish my nursing degree."

"I heard from a buddy of mine that those programs can be hard to get into," he said. "I can see why she wouldn't want you to drop everything in your life to take care of her."

Nora gave him a watery smile. "That's what she said. As soon as my last final was over, I returned to my hometown. I became her nurse. She lasted another three months before she slipped away."

"That's when you joined the Army?"

She shook her head. "Dad was so heartbroken, I stayed a few months until he was feeling better. I got a job at a local emergency room. On weekends, my father and I worked on cleaning out the house and getting it ready to put on the market."

"Is your dad still alive?" Rucker asked.

Nora nodded. "He lives in Texas. He moved to a small house with a big backyard." She forced a smile. "He has a garden, and all the ladies in his retirement community think he's the cat's meow. He still misses Mom, but he's getting on with his life."

Rucker tilted his head. "When did you join the military?"

"When Dad sold the house and moved into his retirement community. I worried about him, but he's doing better."

"And you?"

"I miss her. But she'd whip my ass if I wallowed in self-pity for more than a moment. She was a strong woman and expected me to be the same."

Rucker grinned. "From what I've seen, you are."

Nora gave him a skeptical look. "You've only seen me playing volleyball. It's just a game." Not that she'd admit it, but she was a real softy when it came to caring for the sick and injured.

"If you're half as good at nursing, which I'm willing to bet you are, you're amazing." He started to reach across the table for her hand. Before he actually touched her, he grabbed the saltshaker and shook it over his cold breakfast.

"You just got in this morning?" Nora asked.

Rucker nodded.

"How long will you be here?" she asked.

"I don't know."

"What do you mean, you don't know? I thought when people were deployed, they were given a specific timeframe."

"Most people are. We're deployed where and when needed."

Nora frowned. "What are you? Some kind of special forces team?"

His lips pressed together. "Can't say."

She sat back. He was some kind of Special Forces. "Army, right?"

He nodded.

That would make him Delta Force. The elite of the elite. A very skilled soldier who undertook incredibly dangerous missions. She gulped and stopped herself from reaching across the table to take his hand. "Well, I hope all goes well while you and your team are here."

"Thanks."

A man hurried across the chow hall wearing shorts and an Army T-shirt. He headed directly toward their table.

Nora didn't recognize him. "Expecting someone?" she asked Rucker, tipping her head toward the man.

Rucker turned, a frown pulling his eyebrows together. "Why the hell's Dash awake?"

Nora frowned. "Dash? Please tell me that's his callsign, not his real name."

Rucker laughed. "It should be his real name. He's first into the fight, and he's fast." Rucker stood and faced his teammate. "What's up?"

"CO wants us all in the Tactical Operations Center," Dash said. "On the double."

"Guess that's my cue to exit." Rucker turned to Nora. "I enjoyed our talk."

She nodded. "Me, too."

Dash grinned. "Tell you what…I'll stay and finish your conversation while you see what the commander wants."

Rucker hooked Dash's arm twisted it up behind his back, and gave him a shove toward the door. "You heard the CO, he wants all of us." Rucker winked at Nora. "I hope to see you on the volleyball court before you leave."

"Same. Good luck." Nora's gaze followed Rucker's broad shoulders and tight ass out of the chow hall. Too bad she'd only be there another week before she shipped out. She would've enjoyed more volleyball and coffee with the Delta Force operative.

He'd probably be on maneuvers that entire week.

She stacked her tray and coffee cup in the collection area and left the chow hall, heading for the building where she shared her quarters with Beth Drennan, a nurse she'd become friends with during their deployment together.

As close as they were, Nora didn't bring up her conversation with the Delta. With only a week left at the base, she probably wouldn't run into him again. Though she would like to see him again, she prayed he didn't end up in the hospital.

Breaking Silence

ABOUT THE AUTHOR

ELLE JAMES also writing as MYLA JACKSON is a *New York Times* and *USA Today* Bestselling author of books including cowboys, intrigues and paranormal adventures that keep her readers on the edges of their seats. When she's not at her computer, she's traveling, snow skiing, boating, or riding her ATV, dreaming up new stories. Learn more about Elle James at www.ellejames.com

Website | Facebook | Twitter | GoodReads | Newsletter | BookBub | Amazon

Or visit her alter ego Myla Jackson at mylajackson.com
Website | Facebook | Twitter | Newsletter

Follow Me!
www.ellejames.com
ellejames@ellejames.com

ALSO BY ELLE JAMES

Brotherhood Protectors Colorado

SEAL Salvation (#1)

Rocky Mountain Rescue (#2)

Ranger Redemption (#3)

Tactical Takeover (#4)

Delta Force Strong

Ivy's Delta (Delta Force 3 Crossover)

Breaking Silence (#1)

Breaking Rules (#2)

Breaking Away (#3)

Breaking Free (#4)

Breaking Hearts (#5) coming soon

Iron Horse Legacy

Soldier's Duty (#1)

Ranger's Baby (#2)

Marine's Promise (#3)

SEAL's Vow (#4)

Warrior's Resolve (#5)

Brotherhood Protectors Series

Montana SEAL (#1)

Bride Protector SEAL (#2)

Montana D-Force (#3)

Cowboy D-Force (#4)

Montana Ranger (#5)

Montana Dog Soldier (#6)

Montana SEAL Daddy (#7)

Montana Ranger's Wedding Vow (#8)

Montana SEAL Undercover Daddy (#9)

Cape Cod SEAL Rescue (#10)

Montana SEAL Friendly Fire (#11)

Montana SEAL's Mail-Order Bride (#12)

SEAL Justice (#13)

Ranger Creed (#14)

Delta Force Rescue (#15)

Dog Days of Christmas (#16)

Montana Rescue (Sleeper SEAL)

Hot SEAL Salty Dog (SEALs in Paradise)

Hot SEAL Bachelor Party (SEALs in Paradise)

Brotherhood Protectors Vol 1

The Outrider Series

Homicide at Whiskey Gulch (#1)

Hideout at Whiskey Gulch (#2)

Hellfire Series

Hellfire, Texas (#1)

Justice Burning (#2)

Smoldering Desire (#3)

Hellfire in High Heels (#4)

Playing With Fire (#5)

Up in Flames (#6)

Total Meltdown (#7)

Take No Prisoners Series

SEAL's Honor (#1)

SEAL'S Desire (#2)

SEAL's Embrace (#3)

SEAL's Obsession (#4)

SEAL's Proposal (#5)

SEAL's Seduction (#6)

SEAL'S Defiance (#7)

SEAL's Deception (#8)

SEAL's Deliverance (#9)

SEAL's Ultimate Challenge (#10)

Billionaire Online Dating Service

The Billionaire Husband Test (#1)

The Billionaire Cinderella Test (#2)

The Billionaire Bride Test (#3)

The Billionaire Daddy Test (#4)

The Billionaire Matchmaker Test (#5)

The Billionaire Glitch Date (#6)

The Billionaire Perfect Date (#7) coming soon

The Billionaire Replacement Date (#8) coming soon

The Billionaire Wedding Date (#9) coming soon

Hearts & Heroes Series

Wyatt's War (#1)

Mack's Witness (#2)

Ronin's Return (#3)

Sam's Surrender (#4)

Cajun Magic Mystery Series

Voodoo on the Bayou (#1)

Voodoo for Two (#2)

Deja Voodoo (#3)

Cajun Magic Mysteries Books 1-3

Texas Billionaire Club

Tarzan & Janine (#1)

Something To Talk About (#2)

Who's Your Daddy (#3)

Love & War (#4)

Declan's Defenders

Marine Force Recon (#1)

Show of Force (#2)

Full Force (#3)

Driving Force (#4)

Tactical Force (#5)

Disruptive Force (#6)

Mission: Six

One Intrepid SEAL

Two Dauntless Hearts

Three Courageous Words

Four Relentless Days

Five Ways to Surrender

Six Minutes to Midnight

Ballistic Cowboy

Hot Combat (#1)

Hot Target (#2)

Hot Zone (#3)

Hot Velocity (#4)

SEAL Of My Own

Navy SEAL Survival

Navy SEAL Captive

Navy SEAL To Die For

Navy SEAL Six Pack

Devil's Shroud Series

Deadly Reckoning (#1)

Deadly Engagement (#2)

Deadly Liaisons (#3)

Deadly Allure (#4)

Deadly Obsession (#5)

Deadly Fall (#6)

Thunder Horse Series

Hostage to Thunder Horse (#1)

Thunder Horse Heritage (#2)

Thunder Horse Redemption (#3)

Christmas at Thunder Horse Ranch (#4)

Demon Series

Hot Demon Nights (#1)

Demon's Embrace (#2)

Tempting the Demon (#3)

Lords of the Underworld

Witch's Initiation (#1)

Witch's Seduction (#2)

The Witch's Desire (#3)

Possessing the Witch (#4)

Stealth Operations Specialists (SOS)

Nick of Time

Alaskan Fantasy

Boys Behaving Badly Anthology

Rogues (#1)

Blue Collar (#2)

Pirates (#3)

Stranded (#4)

First Responder (#5)

Blown Away

Warrior's Conquest

Enslaved by the Viking Short Story

Conquests

Smokin' Hot Firemen

Protecting the Colton Bride

Protecting the Colton Bride & Colton's Cowboy Code

Heir to Murder

Secret Service Rescue

High Octane Heroes

Haunted

Engaged with the Boss

Cowboy Brigade

Time Raiders: The Whisper

Bundle of Trouble

Killer Body

Operation XOXO

An Unexpected Clue

Baby Bling

Under Suspicion, With Child

Texas-Size Secrets

Cowboy Sanctuary

Lakota Baby

Dakota Meltdown

Beneath the Texas Moon

CPSIA information can be obtained
at www.ICGtesting.com
Printed in the USA
LVHW011644230321
682230LV00011B/1242

9 781626 953529